ONCE
WE WERE
MAGIC

A NOVEL

"I don't understand why people say,
'I don't want to live forever.'
Why not?" – Alan Alda

Other Novels By Mark Leysen

The Klown

HOA**HOLES

Flemish Fries

A TRAVELING SHOES PRESS BOOK

ONCE
WE WERE
MAGIC

A NOVEL

MARK LEYSEN

TSP

TRAVELING SHOES PRESS
PO BOX 332
Pioneertown, CA 92268

Once We Were Magic
ISBN# 978-1-732-92054-5

First Edition | 2020
Edited by Jeff Edits
Book design by Jon Christopher

Dedicated to Sherry,
the true love of my life.

CONTENTS

1. SAINTLY INVITATION

At five foot nine, she was the tallest girl in class. Top that off with a couple inches of perfectly coiffed bouffant, and she struck quite the figure. Poised and reserved, she was from Minneapolis, a city I didn't know anything about. This was many decades before *Fargo* or the fictional *Lake Wobegon*. She wasn't Norwegian, but she was a Lutheran.

She was in my evening community college hand lettering class; an actual job description in a day when people could earn a living making signs on shop windows, truck cabs, sides of vans, and billboards. I learned she already had a job at a big, Long Beach downtown department store doing display signage. For me, I was looking to learn the craft as a potential side business, being already employed at an interior design studio.

In class, we sat at big wooden drafting desks, hers a row over from mine. I wondered how to attract her attention. One night, I sucked in my breath, crossed my fingers, and wandered up to her desk.

"Wow, your lettering is really good. I'm Garrett, and you?"

"Stella," she smiled, her cornflower blue eyes flashing.

I was hooked. She did two things to me simultaneously: increased my heart rate and put me into a state of serene well-being. I wanted to be with her.

"How about you...the lettering, I mean...how's it coming along?" she asked.

"Come take a look."

When she got up from her drafting stool, I had to stifle the urge to hold her hand and lead her to my desk — after all, we'd just met. I tried to imagine what her hand would feel like.

She leaned over to inspect my work. "Not bad, you're good."

"But not as pro as yours."

She didn't reply, smiled, and went back to her desk.

The class met twice a week, Tuesdays and Thursdays, and on the rare occasion when she didn't make it, I was in an emotional turmoil. I needed to see Stella in place to make my evening right. Although she knew other people in class, I began to more or less place myself into her little group during break at the vending machine.

One night I overheard her say, "...I got so sick from standing at the bus stop, wearing jeans under my skirt to keep from freezing."

"You didn't have a car?"

"I did, but no one drove downtown in the middle of winter to hassle all that snow when you can ride the bus."

"Stella, where did this take place?" I inserted myself into the conversation.

"Minneapolis. I did not want to spend one more winter there. You need to install snow tires on your car, put in different oil, and on really cold nights, run a cable with a turned-on shop light set on top of the engine block so it doesn't freeze and crack."

"Wow, that's a lot of trouble," I said.

"Exactly, which is why I'm here in sunny California."

Our instructor was literally a Saint, and by that, I mean his name was Edward Saint. He noticed that I was focusing my attention on Stella during breaks, plus glancing her way whenever I could.

One evening, Saint handpicked six students to come with him after class to have drinks at a jazz club in Santa Ana. Stella and I were on his list. I was jazzed (pun intended), but at the same time in a near panic. I was not yet twenty-one, which I figured Stella and the others were, or they wouldn't have accepted the invitation.

2. A KISS

We each left campus in our own cars and I followed Stella in her gold-colored 2-seater Triumph. To me, it seemed like a really unique car choice for a young woman, when most of us drove Chevys or Fords. My stomach clenched as I neared the jazz club, afraid that I'd have to sit there and sip a damn root beer while everyone knocked back cocktails. Would Stella consider me potential boyfriend material if she discovered I was underage?

Once inside, Saint took over, finding a large horseshoe shaped booth and basically assigning seating, putting me right next to Stella. On one hand, I couldn't have wished for more, on the other, it heightened my nervous factor that I could be outed as a twenty-year old.

The waitress came to take our orders, and most went for the heavy stuff like highballs and daiquiris, but Stella asked for a beer.

"Me too," I said, hoping the quiver in my voice didn't give me away.

The waitress nodded, and off she went.

I'd passed. Now I was fully in Stella's aura, ready to talk, about what I can't remember, but the evening passed by all too quickly. The jazz was mellow and made for a perfect background, unlike the future amped-up electronic blasts that made you realize why so many our age wear hearing aids. Maybe it was too much of a good thing?

With the jazz club "date" behind us, I realized I was now ready to ask for a solo outing, minus classmates and our Saint of an instructor. She said yes, and again after the evening session, we got into our individual cars and met at a place I'd picked called the Blue Beat, steps away from the Newport Pier. There was dark beer on tap, onion rings to snack on, plus an acoustic folk-rock trio singing about the *Sloop John B* and guys drinking all night and getting into a fight. If it didn't seem so ridiculously out of place, I would have asked Stella to go steady on the spot- yet I hadn't even kissed her.

We weren't there to get drunk, so after two beers, we bid each other good night and she told me she only lived about a mile north on 51st Street.

"I had a good time. Even though I practically live around the corner, I've never been to the Blue Beat. See you in class."

I have to tell you, I've never been shy around girls, but something stopped me from going for that first-night-out kiss. I'm pretty sure Stella would've considered it too early, and I didn't want to spoil the moment. It was perfect as it was.

Karl, one of my body surfing buddies had recently gotten married and wanted to know if I'd like to go on a double date with him and his wife, Nancy. He worked as a writer in the entertainment/restaurant section of our local newspaper and was always getting the scoop on the latest "hot" or "cool" happening place. In this case, it was a pizza joint in LA called Mr. Cheez! (with an exclamation point).

We arrived at a very busy and noisy establishment where a DJ held court like a judge from behind a raised platform, spinning discs, cracking wise, making amplified sound effects over a mike, and taking the time to remark on women's body parts. It was all about tits and ass, and it was 1965. And the pizza was good.

The year before, I'd spent the summer in Europe at the invitation of my father. Not known to be generous about departing with his money, I was told to pay rent when I turned eighteen. I didn't pay up, but moved out, bouncing around at a bunch of low paying jobs: dishwasher, bus boy, and handyman assistant, until I lucked into an interior design studio position. I found it hard to believe my father would pay for my trip, hotel stays, and food with the exception of beer drinking. He was a teetotaler and I could hardly expect him to cover my tab while slurping up delicious European beer at the local bistro. I wondered what the catch was. It was simple.

He'd buy a Mercedes and I'd be the family chauffeur.

So now in the midst of the din at Mr. Cheez!, I was attempting to give Stella highlights of my trip, and perhaps impress her with my worldly travels through major cities like Amsterdam, Paris, Barcelona, and Venice, but it mostly got lost in the cacophony.

"Did you say Paris? Wow, I'd love to go there someday," she said, her warm inviting breath on my cheek.

"We could go together," I said hopefully, although I couldn't tell if she'd heard.

Leaving the parking lot on the way home, Karl flashed me a knowing look in his rearview, hit the gas, and took a sharp accelerated corner, tossing Stella into my lap. I didn't need any more encouragement than that. I kissed her, she kissed me, and that's what we did for the rest of the trip, which, from Hollywood to Newport Beach, takes about an hour.

The magic began.

3. CHANGE OF PLANS

I'd turned twenty-one about a week before our Mr. Cheez! outing, and had been more than happy to pass muster at the ID checking station. There would be no potentially embarrassing moment in front of Stella by a surly security guard saying I wasn't old enough. Happily running that evening over in my mind, I went to the mailbox. Like the proverbial ton of bricks, I got hit by the worst news ever.

My draft notice.

I'd been body surfing and board surfing since I turned fifteen, and had no real hope I'd be rated 4F. I was pretty sure I was the kind of physical specimen the Army was looking for to feed the war machine in Nam. At the induction center, the guy next to me was so nervous he was unable to pee in the sample jar at the urinal.

"Will you do it for me?" he asked.

"Sure, why not, I got plenty for both of us."

The outcome could be one of two. We'd both fail for some medical reason or we'd both get in. We passed, and to this day, I always wonder what happened to him. There was a scary moment when an NCO stepped up to a pile of brown packets and said, "This is your paperwork. When I call your name, come up and take it. Don't fucking lose it!" He waited for the murmuring to settle down. "Now, I'll let you in on a little secret, it seems the goddamn jarheads are a bit short of manpower. So, to help them out, every fifteenth packet will be orders to join the Marines. Good luck with that!"

No way was I Marine Corps material. If I was one of those

"every fifteenth" unlucky bastards, I'd hitchhike home, get in my car, and drive to Canada. Truly!

In class when I broke the news to Stella that I was Army bound, I asked if any of her family had been in the army. She told me her brother was 4F due to poor vision and her father had missed WWII induction coincidentally also due to vision, but caused by a child-hood accident. During the Depression, he'd gone to the railroad tracks to gather chunks of coal that fell off from passing trains. An older kid, competing for the coal, tossed a lump at him and struck his face. It left him permanently blinded in one eye.

Then she mentioned off-hand that while she was in Minneapolis, she'd dated a guy in the Army stationed at Ft. Snelling. I hate hear-ing girls' stories about previous boyfriends, but asked anyway with a tight feeling in the pit of my stomach, "What happened?"

"He assumed we were going to get married and without telling me, rented an apartment, filled it with furniture, and one day, asked me up to see it. He gave me the key and said to open the door. I did. He turns to me, 'It's ours, baby, we'll get married soon as we can.' Obviously, that didn't happen. I packed and moved to California, and here we are."

Maybe Stella left behind both an overbearing winter and boy-friend. A woman hates to be taken for granted.

The semester was three weeks from ending and I told Saint I would not be able to complete it.

"Why?"

"Got drafted."

"Come into my office and let's talk." On the walls were various samples of student work, including my own. "Well, I served in Korea and it was the shits. I don't imagine Vietnam is going to be any better. Look, I'll mark you present on the roll and give you an 'A.' You and Stella are my best students."

"Day after tomorrow, I'm headed for Basic Training."

"To where?"

"Up north. Fort Ord I presume, since it's in California."

"Write to Stella...a lot. You don't want to let go of her."

Magic Words from the Saint.

About 200 of us gathered at the Santa Ana Induction Center, waiting to be bussed to Fort Ord when an NCO in starched fatigues stepped forward. He growled, "Change of plans. You're being transported to the LA Airport and from there, it's on a plane to Fort Polk!"

"Where the fuck is that, Sarge?!" someone shouted from behind me.

He crossed his arms and said, "It's the butthole of America in Louisiana where every other snake is poisonous. I'll only be going with you as far as the airport. Now, form a single line outside. A through L on bus #1, and M through Z on bus #2. Get a fucking move on. Go, go, go!" My last name is DeWalt and I lined up at bus #1. Stella had offered to drive me to the Army Induction Center, but I knew that saying goodbye there would be too heart wrenching, and I hated the thought of crying in front of all the other future grunts. The sight of Stella sitting curbside in her car would be too much to bear. Instead, we said our intimate and prolonged farewell the night before at her apartment.

And that was magic.

Karl drove me and his parting words were, "Don't let the bastards get you down, man."

4. BASIC MOVES

Arriving at the airport in Louisiana, a black sergeant greeted us on the tarmac in front of a cattle truck. "Get your asses inside. Hurry the fuck up! The Army waits for no man!"

The first thing that struck me, physically, was the humidity. In the next edition of Webster's, the definition of humidity should be two words: *Fort Polk*. We were trucked through the base right up to the barber shop. I use the word "barber" loosely. Three chairs awaited us, with hair on the floor up to our ankles. There was no observation of hair styles or making jokes about "a little off the top please" because these guys just cut till there was nothing left. We were given a total buzz before that style later became popular with the hip tattooed crowd, and of course, for us, it was involuntary. The buzz marked you as the lowest of the low, a fresh recruit with no chevrons, referred to as a "slick sleeve."

Next, we were marched to supply and issued our clothes and gear which stuffed into a duffel bag weighed 65 pounds. One fairly small recruit, lugging his duffel up the cattle truck ramp, toppled over backwards. Everyone laughed.

We were assigned to barracks where the row toilets were stainless steel with no lids or partitions. Some recruits couldn't bear the idea of taking a dump while sitting elbow to elbow next to someone, and waited until the dead of the night to dash down to do their business, hopefully minus any company. One joker crumpled up a newspaper sheet, lit it with his Zippo, and let the fireball float downstream the toilet trough, singeing a few butts along the way. As a reward, we organized a blanket party the next night. A blanket was thrown over the sleeping recruit and a half dozen guys pummeled the daylights out of him. He never knew who hit him.

I won't bore you with the day to day details of surviving basic training, except that we did a lot of marching, running, drilling, test taking, shooting, and also standing around doing nothing. One of the Army sayings is: Hurry up and wait.

I wrote to Stella twice a week and tried my best to keep the tone light, funny (like Reader's Digest Humor in Uniform), always ending with how much I loved and missed her. Her married brother and wife from Minneapolis came to visit and she wrote about taking them to Disneyland, Knotts Berry Farm (she'd once worked there briefly on arrival), and the beach where her brother lost his glasses splashing around in the surf. I guess he didn't realize, unlike a lake, the ocean has waves.

Morning mail call was the highlight of my week because I could always count on letters from Stella. A bit of magic to liven up the dreary repetitiveness of basic training, all done under Louisiana's oppressive humidity.

Out in the field practicing with dummy hand grenades, a recruit was messing around doing an impromptu performance. He put on sunglasses, lit a cigarette, and held the grenade to his mouth pretending he was going to pull the ring out with his teeth.

"Look at me, guys, I'm John Wayne."

Our steely-eyed DI marched over. "I'm going to tell you a couple of things, asshole. First of all, if you tried that dumbass move by extracting the ring with your teeth, you'd remove your jaw. Second, John Wayne was never in the Army, only pretended to be in the movies. Third, everything you do here in basic over the course of eight weeks is a test. That means if you fail, you repeat. That's right! The whole goddamn eight weeks you will do all over from day one. You hear me, motherfucker?!"

"Yes, Sergeant."

"What? I can't hear you, boy!"

"YES, SERGEANT!"

"Now ditch those fucking sunglasses and field strip your damn cigarette."

It wasn't just the crushing idea of having to repeat the whole basic routine, but also the potential eight-week attachment afterwards of doing AIT (Advanced Infantry Training). Finished with Basic, we'd get one-week leave and be assigned to our new post which for many, we heard, would be AIT at Ft. Bliss. And as our DI liked to say, "Ft. Bliss ain't no bliss."

Ultimately, the plan was to prepare us for Vietnam, a place we knew very little about except that there was some bad shit going down.

5. A MONKEE

Well, I passed Basic, the John Wayne recruit did not, and when I received my orders, I was beside myself with joy not to have to do AIT. My posting listed: Cameron Station, Exhibit Unit, Alexandria, Virginia.

"What the hell is Cameron Station?" I asked the NCO.

"Fuck if I know. But...Alexandria is across the Potomac from Washington D.C." He drew a blank look. "Exhibit Unit? No damn, idea. Wait. Maybe you're assigned to one of those units that stands guard at the Tomb of the Unknown Soldier. Pure spit-and-polish detail. Those guys even shine the bottoms of their shoes. Good luck, DeWalt. Ha!"

Shining the bottoms of my shoes? If ever there ever was someone who wasn't spit-and-polish, it was US Army Pfc. Garrett DeWalt.

In uniform, a soldier could fly at half price on standby, and since it was a midday flight to LA, I got on immediately. I'd called Karl to pick me up and he met me at the airport.

"Where to buddy?"

"Stella's. She got a new place in Huntington Beach, right by the pier."

It wasn't exactly a *new place* but rather a different place. I gave him the address and an hour later, I was dropped off in front of a sagging, two-story shingle roof, wood framed house with an actual porch. I guessed it was built pre-World War II by decades because after the war, builders in a rush to construct tract homes by the thousands decided that porches were no longer necessary. After dinner, people didn't sit out front anymore, they got into their car and drove somewhere. Anywhere to escape the sameness of their neighborhoods and momentarily forget their upcoming mortgage payment.

My heart warmed immediately at the sight of a beautiful hand-lettered sign on brown butcher paper hung in the front window. One word was all it took: WELCOME!

I knocked on the door and Stella's roommate, Dora, answered.

She stared at my head. "Oh...my...god...what happened to your... hair?"

"Got cut."

"The uniform's not bad, though. Stella's at the beach. Come in and I'll show you her room. You can change and," she pointed at my duffel bag, "put that thing away."

I'd left a few of my civilian clothes with Stella, and I couldn't change fast enough to get into my bright orange trunks, T-shirt, and flip flops. The house was one block from Pacific Coast Highway, and I jaywalked across, too much of a hurry to go up the street to use the crosswalk. I quickly spotted Stella. She was reading, and I let my eyes take in her gorgeous, perfectly tanned, lanky body stretched across a beach towel in a flower-patterned bikini. After eight weeks in fatigues, I was as white as a sheet and with my GI haircut, I felt like a Rube, not the beach person I once was. I must have stood there just staring, taking in her presence, knowing she was my girlfriend.

It was a magical feeling.

I hoofed it down to where she was and approached, "Hi, darling."

Stella shielded her eyes from the sun and was polite enough not to remark on my haircut or lack of a tan. She patted her towel, "Sit." I did, and we kissed. I would have loved to pick her up and carry her across the sand, the highway, to her house up the stairs into her bedroom, but...one must be patient.

Stella had landed a side job creating hand-lettered signs at a place called the Golden Bear, a five-minute walk from her house. At that time, it was mostly a folk-rock venue, which would later morph into a very well-known rock spot featuring among others, Janis Joplin, Jimi Hendrix, and the Doors. Currently on stage was Jose Feliciano, a blind, Puerto Rican singer guitarist, plus Ian and Sylvia, a married duo from Canada. We loved the couple's bluesy folk-rock sound, and bought their album, our first LP record purchase together.

Stella gave me the inside scoop about them. Performing together, Ian and Sylvia were totally in sync, harmonizing, making great music. But once backstage, they turned into the Bickersons, disagreeing about almost everything. Years later, they divorced.

That night, as I made it across the threadbare carpet of Stella's house en route to the bathroom, I bumped into a gangly guy. Like myself, he was in his underwear.

"Who are you?" we both said.

"I'm Dora's boyfriend, Peter."

"I'm Stella's boyfriend, Garrett."

"Oh, yeah, Stella, she's sweet, does all the cool signage at the Golden Bear where I work."

"Are you a musician?"

"Someday, man. Right now, I'm the dishwasher at the Golden Bear. And, you're the Army guy."

"Not by choice."

Little did Stella and I, or Dora, know that someday he'd become famous as one of the Monkees. Even with their hit TV series and number one song *Last Train to Clarksville*, the group was not exactly loved by everyone. About a year later, while I grabbed a coffee in my army dayroom, a fellow soldier said, "I told my girlfriend that if I catch her watching the Monkees, I'll toss the damn TV set out of the window. And we live on the fourth floor." Most everyone applauded.

Due to the complexity and expense of seismic retrofitting, the Golden Bear was torn down in 1986 and a lot of magic was lost.

6. LOOKING BUSY

I arrived at Cameron Station and signed into the Exhibit Unit, only to discover there were no barracks on base or living quarters for any military personnel. Instead we would "live on the economy" as the military term described it. It also meant no free mess hall meals or a place to sleep. Temporarily, I grabbed the cheapest downtown hotel I could find. All the other GIs split rent by rooming two to three per apartment, but I didn't know anyone yet and there were no posted bulletin board vacancies.

The hotel clerk would give me a reduced rate of two and a half dollars, down from three bucks a day, if I paid upfront for two weeks. I did, figuring by then I'd find someone who had a room to rent. I wrote to Stella to give her my Duke Street hotel address and spent my first weekend wandering around Old Town Alexandria with my sketch book, drawing old building facades. According to brass plaques, George Washington had patronized some of the former drinking establishments, which supposedly served ale in glass-bottomed tankards so they could see the Brits coming while merrily imbibing.

For some reason, my arrival at the Exhibit Unit was unexpected. Another soldier from New York had the same scheduled check-in time as me, but there didn't seem to be a slot or desk for me. I sat in the XO's office as he pored over my paperwork. My stomach clenched at the thought he might say: *Well, DeWalt, we can always send you to Vietnam, they need more live bodies there.*

Lt. Colonel Sandro Barone, the XO, peered over my papers.

"Says here that you attended Orange Grove Community College. Never heard of it. Hold on." He reached for a fat, green hardback directory on his desk and thumbed through it. "Hmm, according to this it's an *agricultural* college." He looked at me as if he expected me to be chewing on a strand of hay.

"*Was*, sir."

"What?"

"In 1960, the agricultural part was dropped. It's a regular college like any other. You most likely have an outdated reference, sir." He didn't seem really happy being told his big book wasn't current.

"Regardless, DeWalt, these orders definitely have you in our pipeline, yet I've received no specific notification of where to slot you in. You are an art major?"

"Yes, sir."

He leaned back in his leather swivel chair and pointed to a framed print on the wall. "Who's that painted by?"

"Claude Monet, sir, titled *River Scene Bennecourt, Seine*. It shows his future wife Camille, who has her back turned to the viewer so as not to reveal she was pregnant."

"I see...and that one?"

"By Pissarro, *Boulevard Montmartre*. Of all the Impressionists, he was the least successful financially, and ironically, his first name was also Camille like Monet's would-be wife and -"

"Enough, DeWalt. Obviously, you know something about art. Let's march you over to Art&Design, pronto. I'll introduce you to Sergeant Schleyer, and it'll be his damn problem what the hell to do with you."

Schleyer's problem was to find me a desk, when none were available. He scribbled a note, handed it to me, and said, "Go see Gutierrez in Supply."

I walked to the back of the warehouse to patiently wait out Sergeant Gutierrez regaling his supply cohorts with a lengthy joke about a farmer, a sheep, and a traveling salesman. After the laughter abated, he turned to me and barked, "What the fuck do you want...DeWalt?"

I slid the note across his battered counter.

"A desk! Hey guys, he wants a damn desk!"

Everyone broke up like it was even funnier than the farmer joke. I stood cooling my heels for another minute, until Gutierrez finally opened the bottom of the Dutch door next to the counter to let me in. "Yo, Jesse, go help find this asshole a desk, and square him away with his artbox."

Jesse was black, one of only two in the Exhibit Unit, other than a front desk sergeant months away from retiring. Harry Truman may have integrated the Army, but there wasn't a lot of evidence of it at our unit. We were staffed by 80 enlisted, four officers, four WACS, and five civilians - one of them a female secretary.

My "desk" turned out to be a rickety wooden table like something you might find in a slum kitchen apartment, but it was mine. I half expected to open the drawer and find a greasy butter knife. I helped Jesse put my desk on a trolley and we wheeled it into Art&Design. Schleyer took a look at it, shook his head, and had it shoved into a corner, which surprisingly came with an unused cork board. From my lowly vantage point, I could look up at nearly a dozen soldier/artists doing who knows what at their pro, slant-top, adjustable drafting desks with attached brushed aluminum swivel lamps. No lamp for me.

Schleyer wagged his chin at me. "Look DeWalt, I don't have anything for you to do, but for shit's sake look busy."

Believe me, that was not a difficult request to fill. One thing that has always flowed naturally from the tip of my pen, is the ability to draw cartoons. I had to take two semesters of lettering to learn the craft, but no instructor needed to show me how to make cartoons. I started drawing like a madman, pinning up my work, waiting for some magic to happen.

7. ABC RULES

A little bit of magic came in the form of a short, stocky, New York-accented soldier called Jake Block who offered me a room in a unique historical place I'd never heard of called the Thompson Building. Finally, a room of my own and not in a seedy hotel with a metal spring mattress, a sink, and no toilet. Jake was an architectural draftsman and, in his bedroom, had hand-built a drawing desk topped by a loft bed, accessible by ladder. The ceiling was easily 18-feet high, which left plenty of headroom above my upper tier bed. I loved it.

Jake had three days to go before his army time was over and he introduced me to my future roommate, Alberto (Al) Vicente, a guy in desperate need of a shave at mid-afternoon. He wasn't sporting a five o'clock shadow, but was already in full bloom of a heavy three o'clock shadow. Al worked in the silkscreen shop and was pleasant enough, with the minor exception of being a devout Catholic who regularly attended mass, didn't drink, and hung a large, black and white framed photo of a stern-faced Pope Paul VI in the hall. We each had our own bedroom, but it was the first time since I'd left home that I had to share living quarters with another person, not counting the brief, magical week snuggled up with Stella in her seaside bed.

Al, being Italian, did not mind doing the cooking, which was fine by me. We ate a lot of spaghetti, tomato soup, eggplant parmesan, chicken cacciatore, and various pastas only an Italian would know the name of. My job was to clean up.

"Al, I have to ask. I've been at our unit for nearly four weeks and I have no goddamn idea what we do."

"First of all, please don't use God's name in vain, and do you have to drink beer with every meal?"

"Beer enhances your delicious cuisine."

He exhaled sharply. "I can't believe no one told you what our unit's mission is."

"Well, not in so many words. Clue me in."

"We, at the unit, are responsible for conceptualizing, designing, manufacturing, and outfitting exhibits that promote the US Army. We have two eighteen-wheelers that we outfit with custom-made exhibits to tour around the US that civilians can view for free. Our trucks make appearances at State and County Fairs, City Hall Events, and even at mall openings."

"That clears things up, and I better clean things up here because I don't have too much time left until the Royal closes. No one told me Virginia is a dry state and the cafes close at midnight."

If you wanted something stronger than beer or wine, a trip to the local ABC outlet was required. There, you were greeted by a guy in a white lab coat at a counter, not unlike a pharmacist, ready to fill your prescription. Behind him were shelves and shelves of liquor that you were not allowed to meander through, but only view a typed, alphabetical list posted on the wall from which to choose. It really took all the fun out of buying booze, and I'm an infrequent consumer at that. As an artist, I always enjoy looking at label design, typography (especially on Russian vodkas), bottle shape, and, of course, alcohol content.

"Give me a pint of Ron Rico rum," I said.

"You got it," the ABC drone answered. "A store down the block sells Coke."

"Thanks, but I'll just drink it straight as I go. You know, where I'm from you can buy liquor at a grocery store or even a drug store."

"And where would that...be?"

"California." That magical state.

"So, why are you here?"

I ran a hand across my still fairly-short Basic Training haircut. "Drafted."

8. GROUND ZERO

I noticed that when an officer came into Art&Design, a soldier would stand up, if directly approached at his desk. Otherwise, you kept your head down and acted busy, like Schleyer ordered me. Lt. Barone arrived at my table, his shoes clacking off the polished cement floor. I stood up and waited for whatever he had to say. He motioned to a soldier a couple of desks in the other direction and said, "Thomas, get your butt over here."

"Yes, sir."

All I knew about Jeff Thomas was that he lived with his parents at home in Arlington, maybe a twenty-minute drive away. No shared apartment for him, instead it was home-cooked food, plus his own bed to sleep in.

"Thomas, I want you to take DeWalt with you on your routes for all of the next week. Show him the ropes, square him away. Got it?"

"Yes, sir."

Lt. Colonel Barone strode off, leaving me to wonder what the brief conversation actually meant. "Routes?" I asked.

Thomas looked at my cork board. "Those cartoons are great. Is that what you did in civilian life?"

"No, I worked at an interior design studio doing renderings of furniture."

"Okay, here's the deal. I'm finishing my Army stay in two weeks and once again will be a civilian. Hooray!" He fist-pumped the air. "As a side job here, I also drive our CO, Colonel Sullivan, plus I make two runs to the Pentagon every day."

"So that's why you're often away from your desk."

"Believe me, it's nice getting out. From now on, you'll have to wear khakis or Army Greens with the tie."

I was in fatigues.

"The good news is they won't put you on a shit detail if you're in class-A Greens. The colonel hates to see a rumpled or paint flecked uniform." Thomas started walking away, "Oh, you do have a driver's license, don't you?"

"Thomas, I'm from California."

"Right, I forgot."

Even then, I had to walk down to Motor Pool and be issued a military driver's license; but no written or driving test was required once I showed my California driver's ID. At Motor Pool, every single soldier was black. I guess that was the Army's local definition of integration. Thomas (we mostly used last names because it was sewn onto our uniforms), turned out to be an effective driving guide who instructed me on the ins and outs of Washington DC's baroque, and often confusing, city layout with angular streets radiating out in unexpected directions.

"The master DC City plan was designed by Pierre L'Enfant," Thomas said. "After that, he didn't do much, and died broke."

Thomas was easy going, which I figure had a lot to do with the fact that he was about to exit the Army after three years. A "short-timer" as it was called.

One of our daily stop offs was the Pentagon. The building was like a whole city embedded into five stories of solid concrete, plus two basement floors. First time Thomas took me there, my thought was: *how the hell will I ever find my way around this behemoth*?

Again, Thomas showed me the way by describing how the office address system worked in connection with the separate floor levels, rings, and corridors. Within a month, I would consider the Pentagon my home away from home. The Concourse had a military clothing store, a bank, a dentist, an airline ticket agency, and everyone's favorite, a bookstore. Once a month, military personnel (all male) would line up out the door for their hotly anticipated new issue of Playboy.

"Man, look at the jugs on Miss April, will ya!"

"Tits? It's her ass I dig!"

Sexism was rampant in military service.

One afternoon as we walked down Corridor 6 to the internal outdoor Pentagonal Plaza, Thomas said, "Even though you're outside, you do not need to wear your hat or salute any officers. The Plaza is five acres, and unofficially called *Ground Zero*."

"Why is that?"

"When the Russians drop the big one, that's what they'll aim for."

I'll never know what hit me as I sit on a sunny bench with my yogurt of the day.

9. SQUARED AWAY

I gave Stella both my Exhibit Unit and new apartment address. I received letters at the apartment on Fairfax, but postcards came to the unit. All were handmade on thick cardboard stock, and were embellished with hand lettering flourishes, sometimes with add-on woodblock printing, plus collage elements and sepia-tone photos she took of herself in photobooths. (The original selfie.) The letters and cards inserted a bit of "Stella Magic" into the uniformity of my army life. Each card was a minor work of art, which is exactly what our company adjutant, Lt. Trent, said. Instead of gathering everyone onto the warehouse floor for mail call, he walked through all the shops and hand delivered to each trooper. He confessed that he really didn't have that much to do, and it was a good way to stretch his legs and get to know all the men.

He looked with admiration at Stella's latest card, making no effort to hide the fact he was reading the back. "I gotta ask, who is this Stella Kalivoda? Is she a Polack, a Russkie, or what?"

"Third-generation Czechoslovakian."

Lt. Trent was an OCTS (Officer Candidate Training School) graduate, or "90-day wonder" as it was disparagingly called. I'd qualified for the program in Basic Training because my test scores were high enough, but I'd declined for one reason: it would mean serving an additional year. Trent was no lifer like the other senior officers and NCOs, and was just as eager to complete his tour as everyone else in Art&Design.

"So, is Stella your steady girl?"

"Yes."

"Too bad she's 3,000 miles away," he chuckled.

"Thanks for reminding me, Lieutenant."

My trial by fire came one early Thursday morning when I had to drive our CO, Colonel Sullivan, to his once weekly Pentagon "strategy meeting." There would be no Thomas in the driver's seat with me tagging along as a passenger. I parked the company car, a four-door blue Ford, at the Exhibit Unit front entrance. Our Topkick, Whittaker, came out and gave me the once over. "Drive like you have a crate of eggs in the backseat. And most of all...don't fuck up!"

I didn't reply as Whittaker left, and stood by the right rear door to pop it open the second Sullivan arrived.

"Morning, Sir," I saluted.

"DeWalt," he saluted back. "Thomas is a civilian again, I see."

"Yes, sir."

I shut his door, went around, jumped behind the wheel, and drove off for the Pentagon. He opened his attaché case and read paperwork for the whole trip. I dropped him off at the West Entrance so he could meet with General Warner in his 2E601 office. Sullivan looked at his watch. "Pick me up at eleven hundred."

"Yes, sir." Having an office in the E-Ring was like having an E-ticket at Disneyland. Not only were General Warner's elaborate suite of offices in the coveted outer ring, but it was in the outer *outer* ring, meaning he had windows to look out of that huge fortress, which came with 17 miles of corridors.

Thomas had told me about "hidden perks" of being the colonel's driver. This was one of them. Other than delivering three envelopes on the same floor, I basically had two hours to do what I wanted and didn't have to account for it. I made it down to the Concourse, stopping off at a snack bar on the way for a bagel, hardboiled egg, and coffee. In the book store, I bought Joseph Heller's *Catch-22*. I'd heard it was a terrific satirical take on the WWII Army Air Corps, which later would become a separate service known as the Air Force.

General Curtis LeMay was head of the Air Force and badly wanted a fifth star like some of the other famous WWII generals, and lobbied President Johnston for it. LBJ did not care for the man and his blunt spoken ways, and refused. General LeMay retired and moved to Newport Beach.

The cashier, a civilian, had read *Catch-22*, and winked, "It's hilarious, you'll dig it, wickedly funny." He leaned in closer, "And you know what's like totally weird? Guess how many times Heller's manuscript was rejected?"

"Twenty-two times?"

"Right on, pal."

I went back to the parking lot, stashed my novel under the seat, not sure if Colonel Sullivan would approve of my anti-war reading choice, and returned to spend the rest of my time browsing, looking at military art on the walls. It was a collection of original oil paintings that had been collected by the Army, some done by civilians and others by combat artists directly in the line of fire. One particular series, which caught the close attention of a group of visiting women, was of Revolutionary officers in their snappy uniforms and tight white breeches. Highly detailed, it was pretty clear to see if a man "wore to the left or right."

At eleven hundred sharp, I stepped up to General Warner's open office door and was waved in by his civilian secretary, whose brass desk name plate identified her as Lorraine Doyle. "Call me Lorrie," she said by way of introduction. "Take a load off, sit down. Your colonel is still wrapped up in his meeting with the general. Coffee?"

"Thanks, but already had some at the snack bar."

She wrinkled her nose at the mention of snack bar. "Well, whenever you're around, it's free here, and tastier."

Coincidently, twenty-two minutes later, Sullivan arrived. "Okay, m'lad, let's head back to the unit."

On the return trip with nothing to read evidently, Sullivan engaged in conversation. (As Thomas and Topkick Whittaker had warned me, only speak when spoken to.) "Barone tells me he wasn't notified of your arrival, yet all your paperwork was in order."

"Yes, sir."

"Well, no matter, you're here and that's fine. With the escalation of the overseas conflict and the President's increased draft numbers, there's bound to be confusion somewhere along the pipeline. Did Schleyer in A&D get you squared away?"

"Indeed, he did, sir." If you can call a broken-down wooden table being squared away. However, I was also issued a cardboard shoebox of random art materials, most likely rejects from the other guys in A&D, but they were mine to use.

I returned to the base, parked in front of the Exhibit Unit, ran around, and let Sullivan out. He nodded and went up the short steps where his civilian secretary, Mary, held the door open. She gave me a thumbs up.

I hadn't fucked up.

10. PUBLISHED

"Hi, I'm Martin Noble and I'm looking for a cartoonist." I had not met this particular Southern-accented soldier in our unit, who was looking at the various drawings and cartoons I'd pinned to my corkboard.

"Cartoons for what, Martin?"

"I'm the editor of our weekly newsletter, the Exhibiteer. Read it?"

I'd looked at it. Four pages of typewriter typesetting with a bold, all-caps headline here or there that didn't make for the most exciting visual layout. But had I read it? No.

"Yes," I said.

"What I'd like is a simple black and white line drawing, no shading. You can use pen and ink or brush. I'll take a Photostat of your cartoon and drop it in." Martin plunked a copy of the Exhibiteer on my table, and pointed. "Make it two columns wide. I'll need your cartoon every Thursday no later than fifteen hundred. Can you do that?"

"Sure." I now had two official jobs, company cartoonist and the colonel's driver, yet nothing to do with what Art&Design was involved with, even though I occupied a space in their section. If they didn't need me, I no longer needed them.

I didn't really know enough about army life in general to whip out cartoons, ala Beetle Bailey (or TV sitcom's scheming Phil Silvers as Sgt Bilko), so I thought I'd concentrate on actual individuals. I started on the guy who gave me the job, Martin Noble, head of

News Release. I made a caricature of him sitting behind his Remington, typewriter ribbon ingloriously spooled out and enmeshed in his blackened fingertips. I had no idea how he'd react.

"Changing his ribbon."

"I fucking love it. What's your overall plan?"

"I'll do some specific individuals, but then change to general observations as I get to know more about the unit. Just the guys going about their daily routine."

Martin eyed me. "How about the officers?"

"I'll toss them in randomly, no specific order."

"How do you think they'll react?"

"We'll find out."

Martin smirked. "*You'll* find out."

My next cartoon victim was Sgt. Morita, head of the metal shop. I depicted him accidentally squirting his fatigue shirt with an oversized oil can. He didn't think it was funny, and told me so. Then came Sgt. Jerry Havelik in the Electric Shop, getting zapped from a wire he was stripping. He thought the cartoon hilarious and pinned it above his workbench. I drew Sgt Ben Hogue, head of the sign shop getting his spelling twisted by printing GO AMRY! No comment from Hogue. Once a year, we had to qualify in the gas chamber with our masks, so that became a topic, and an excercise no one liked. I also joked about the draft seen through the eyes of Santa Claus.

I mailed off clippings of my "published" cartoons to Stella, who replied, "This could be the best job you've ever had."

Possibly it was, with the exception of my salary. My first monthly paycheck was $120 dollars, of which thirty-five went to rent, leaving me just under three bucks per day for food, beer, and a haircut every ten days that Topkick Whittaker insisted we get. He had an innate sense when we weren't in compliance and would sneak up to the back of us, pinch a hank of hair, and growl: "What are you, some kind of goddamn hippie? Get a fucking haircut. NOW!"

One of the ways I supplemented my meager diet was pure sneakery. I'd go to the base cafeteria which had a milk dispenser. I'd fill a glass, turn my back to the cashier, quickly gulp it down, and refill it. Next, I'd go over to the community tables and sit close to a large group because experience told me, people did not always eat everything on their tray, and no one bussed their tables when they vacated. By being selective, I'd score an uneaten roll with a pat of butter, a chicken wing, and the occasional square of scrapple - a new food item to me. I learned that scrapple's composition was pork scraps, cornmeal, and spices, pan fried like a hamburger patty. The South's version of Spam.

Coffee was free, pretty much everywhere I went. There was a giant urn in the front lobby that Sgt. Evans, one of our four WACS (described by Jeff Thomas as "incredibly attractive"), kept topped off all day with a complement of sugar and powdered milk. Occasionally, a box of donuts was brought in exclusively for front office personnel. Since the mailbox I retrieved envelopes for my deliveries was in the front office, I took it upon myself to grab a donut now and then. No one stopped me. Donuts were also served in the day room, as were bear claws and bagels, but you had to pay.

One morning while chowing down on a maple donut, Lt Col. Barone came out of his office to give me a head to toe inspection.

"Son, you need to be outfitted in TWs." He slowly turned to take in the attractive Sgt. Evans. "Don't you think so, Evans?"

"I do indeed, sir."

"Right. He'd look a lot sharper."

I had no idea what the two were going on about.

Barone motioned at Evans. "Why don't you accompany DeWalt back to supply and tell Jesse he needs to be outfitted on the double."

"Yes, sir."

Sgt. Evans explained that TW stood for Tropical Worsted. "Same light-weave fabric that the hip civilians in Florida used to wear back in the 40s and 50s, called a Palm Beach suit. Practically wrinkle-free, and you won't have to wear a tie like your Army Greens."

Best damn uniform I ever had. Tan, comfortable, and like Evans said, near wrinkle proof. Kind of magical.

The Army phased out TW's in the late 1970s.

"Hey Harry, you gonna wear
something green on St. Patty's Day?"

"And do you think it's easy getting a hold of
40,000 competent 19 to 23 year-old elves every year?"

"You'll be moving to LA next week - this'll
be a good excercise for you. HA!"

"Forget about her.
She's a booby trap."

11. POPE PAUL VI

The next letter I got from Stella was a terrific piece of news. She was coming for a visit! (But in a roundabout way.) First, she and her roommate Dora would go on the ultimate road trip, which would beat anything Jack Kerouac had ever accomplished. They'd drive from Huntington Beach up the California Coast, through Oregon, Washington, into Canada over to Calgary, across the vast expanse of Canadian territory (as Gertrude Stein might say: was there anything *there*?), to the Great Lakes, and down into Minneapolis to visit Mom and Dad. Then, on to Chicago where Dora had relatives, leaving the Windy City for Maine, travel south to New York, and from there, to see me in Alexandria. Without making a formal mileage count, I guesstimated the trip to be around 8,000 miles. Two 23-year-olds in a Volkswagen Bug with sleeping bags. If anything, Stella was the most adventurous soul I'd ever met, magical really.

After a week with me in Alexandria, the duo would continue on to Florida and then back home through the South and South West.

Somewhere along the line, I'd have to mention to Al, my staunch Catholic roommate (who'd recently informed me that he was joining the priesthood after finishing his military stint), that I'd be sleeping with my girlfriend in a state of unmarried bliss in my lofty bed. I wasn't sure how he'd react.

Al didn't take it nearly as well I thought he might.

He threw a half-eaten plate of spaghetti against the kitchen wall, right after I brought it up, then stomped away. I could leave it and let the cockroaches make a meal of it, or clean it myself. I finished my spaghetti, mentally daring the damn roaches to come out but they stayed put. They preferred darkness. I washed the mess off, put the broken plate into the trash, and decided now was as good a time as any to paint that wall. Like a lot of things in Old Town Alexandria, it hadn't been touched since the Civil War.

Al returned and half-heartedly apologized. "Sorry...um, oh, you took care of it...I was going to..."

"There's a gallon of white paint from supply that I was going to use to touch up my bedroom, but I'll donate it to paint this section of wall. Let's do it together, now."

"Now?"

"Yes."

Working side by side late into the night may have mellowed Al's opinion a bit, particularly when I said, "I pay an equal share of the rent, so what goes on in the privacy of my bedroom should be no concern of yours. I don't need you to land some Catholic... (I almost started to say 'bullshit') guilt trip on me."

He didn't reply, and kept painting.

"And by the way, Stella and I lived together before I got drafted." Actually, only for a week during my leave from Basic Training, but Al didn't need to be given specifics of our personal life. I could have added it was 1966 and that the country was in the throes of a sexual revolution, and taking the pill was ubiquitous among the young female population.

Next time I passed Pope Paul VI's photo in the hallway, I swore he glared at me and whispered "fornicator." I felt I needed to hang a photo of someone next to the pope's stern visage as a counter balance, but wasn't able to come up with any secular personal hero. I did fleetingly consider the new British actor, Michael Caine, star of *Alfie*, who plays a roguish man about town and has sex with lots of women. But that might have been too blatant a poke in the eye for Al.

12. MILITARY CONDUCT

I counted the days until Stella's arrival and, in anticipation, bought a new set of sheets at JC Penney's. Al liked the one wall we'd painted so much, he bought a new gallon and took it upon himself to do the whole kitchen, or maybe it was the thought of a woman's arrival and potential scrutiny that prompted him.

We had been taking the city bus to the unit, but an upstairs neighbor who was in Art&Design bought a car, suggested we carpool with him. Spec-5 John Tweed was an illustrator, a good friend with Harry Mansker, another illustrator, and the only married man in A&D. Harry's wife was a ticket agent for a major airline at the DC Airport, and he'd been driving her to work, to then swing back and head for the unit. Tweed suggested he join our carpool, leaving the car to his wife, Dena.

Working for an airline, whether as stewardess or ground personnel, female employees were expected to have and maintain a certain "pleasing and shapely figure." Gain a few pounds and one got a reprimand, fine, or even fired. Basically, the women had to look camera-ready for a Playboy layout. Dena did not disappoint; she was a real knockout. My routine in the carpool when we arrived at Harry's two-story townhouse was to run up to the door, knock, and shout, "We're here, let's go." Harry would then dash out and join us for the ride to the unit.

One morning, I didn't shout, and just knocked. The door swung open and there appeared Dena in an open robe, nothing underneath.

My first thought was: *what a lovely life drawing model she'd make.*

"Oh, gosh, sorry. Thought you were Harry and he forgot something." Dena fastened her robe, hardly concerned about the exposure. She pointed down the sidewalk. "There's Harry, he must have gone to the corner for a newspaper."

I smiled, quickly returned to Tweed's car as Harry climbed in. "Meet the wife?" he said, chipper as a jaybird, popping open his Washington Post.

"I did, Harry." With Dena's naked form embedded in my mind, I was all the more eager to have Stella arrive.

Friday mornings were dedicated to a weekly unit meeting in the day room, where every single person, save the civilians, had to gather to listen to Lt. Trent impart some aspect of military conduct. We sat in folding chairs facing the front where Trent was posted at a lectern, with Lt. Colonel Barone, Colonel Sullivan on one side, facing us, along with Sergeant Major Stubbins and Major Trammel. The front row was reserved for the four WACS, who did their best to squeeze knees together to keep Major Trammel's roving eye from going up-skirt. Topkick Whittaker remained standing by the open doorway to shout: "TENSHUN!" as the officers paraded in. We'd all stand and snap to attention, and the process was repeated when the meeting was over. Officers always arrived last, but left first, followed by the WACS.

Today's topic was about NOT joining in any protest marches while in uniform.

"How about out of uniform in civvies?" Martin Noble asked.

"A bit of advice, Martin. If you get arrested, we'll slap an Article 15 on you. Know what that means?"

"Yes, sir, I do. Reduction in rank, a fine, and possible time in the stockade."

"Good. You do know."

"I wasn't planning to join a march, just askin' for the unit's benefit, sir."

Everyone laughed, including the brass.

"Does anyone have a complaint to log in?"

This was the world's most ridiculous question. What soldier in his right mind would lodge a complaint while all officers were present? I'd heard from Martin that before I arrived at the unit, one guy did. He is no longer with us, now humping a rucksack in Nam.

That ended the meeting, and I drove to the Pentagon to deliver various letters, requests, information handouts, and drop off twenty copies of the Exhibiteer.

Some of the paperwork had to be signed, and I'd wait as it was read and returned with a formal signature. Topkick Whittaker had growled, "A telephone call ain't worth the paper it's written on. That's why you get stuff signed off. It's proof whoever's on the other end read the damn document."

13. JOHN LENNON

The day I'd been in high anticipation for finally arrived. I'd left my apartment key in the vestibule mailbox so Stella could let herself in. And there she was, sitting on our stoop in Bermuda's, her bare long legs sticking out, calmly eating cherries from a bowl. I nearly ripped the door off John's car in my rush to get out.

"DeWalt, take it easy, she ain't going anywhere," he shouted.

My heart beat through my chest as we got into a prolonged hug, and remained kissing until John tapped my shoulder. "Come up for air, buddy, and introduce us."

"Stella, this is John Tweed, our attic neighbor, and this is Al Vicente, my roommate."

She was all smiles. "Hi, guys, pleased to meet you."

The four of us stood there a bit awkwardly, not knowing where the conversation should go next, until Al said, "I better get inside and make dinner for three. Oh, John, you're welcome to join us."

"Thanks, but I've got a glass of ale waiting for me at the Royal and a waitress I have my eye on."

Al and John went inside and Stella said, "These buildings are all so old-looking, it's like being in a time warp during George Washington's time."

To impress her with my knowledge, I stated, "Although some are from that period, many are newly constructed to architectural standards that mandate the facades must comply with what is called the Federalist Period."

She nodded. "And you know all this, how?"

"I read that at the library,"

"Here's to the Federalist Period. Want a cherry?"

"Sure. By the way, where's your traveling companion, Dora?"

"Dora decided to, in her words, 'hang back at the Greenwich Village to dig the scene and groove on the cool vibe.' She'll come in a week or so. She ran out of money and got a temporary waitress job at the Bitter End."

Al prepared his signature dish: eggplant parmesan with French beans and garlic bread sticks. As we sat down, Stella snapped her fingers. "I've got the perfect thing to go with this dinner." She quickly left, returned with a bottle of Chianti, and pulled three glasses from the cupboard.

Al waved, "Oh, no, Stella, I don't drink."

She stood over him and rested her hand on his shoulder. "Al, you're Italian, you've just prepared an Italian dish, and wine is what you drink with a meal like this. I'm sure your pope is having a glass right now. Come on." Stella started to pour when I added, "You know Al, in Europe, kids drink wine with dinner, except they cut it in half with water."

"Do you want it that way?" she lightly taunted.

His dark eyes flashed. "No, I'll have the adult portion. Go ahead and fill it."

I'd been trying to get Al to have a glass of beer since the day I moved in without success, yet all it took from Stella was one small nudge and here he was having wine.

Since my bedroom was only separated by a hallway from Al's, we did our best to be as quiet as possible. But in the heat of the moment, it can be hard to hold back.

Next morning as I passed Al on the way to the kitchen, he said rather curtly, "I didn't hear a thing."

For the time that Stella stayed, she drove me to the unit in the mornings, which was noticed by Topkick Whittaker who made it his mission to station himself at the loading ramp where we entered the building. He eyed his watch and if we came in one minute after oh-eight hundred, he would be one pissed-off sergeant, and most likely we'd be assigned a shit detail. Sometimes literally, like painting the latrine stalls.

"Who's the gal in the blue VW Bug?" he asked.

"My girlfriend."

He did a second take as Stella drove off. "Wait a sec. She has California plates. You mean to tell me she drove all the way from fucking California just to see your dumb mug?"

"Yes, Sarge, that's exactly what she did," I omitted it was also part of her around the USA/Canada tour with a roommate.

"You are one lucky sonofabitch."

"Thank you, Sarge."

That evening, surprise, surprise, at Stella's invitation, Al came with us to the Royal. It was something he'd always refused, at my beckoning, due to the fact that he considered it a "den of iniquity." As we got Carling's Ale, to level the field, Al asked for a Schweppes.

The waitress eyed him sharply. "Do you have booze stashed with you?"

Al blinked. "I don't know what you mean."

"Customers come in, order a soda, and when I'm not looking, pour in gin from a flask. It's illegal. Are you gonna do that?"

Both Stella and I cracked up. "Al doesn't drink. (With the exception of one glass of wine with dinner.) And he's going into the priesthood."

She scoffed. "Like they don't drink."

We ordered the fried shrimp boat with sides of onion rings. Fried food, the fuel of the South.

"Al, still think the Royal is filled with lecherous people, lurching about drunkenly?" I teased.

In reality, the Royal Cafe was strictly blue collar. Truck drivers, army personnel, longshoremen, construction workers, plus girlfriends, wives, and a few ladies with perhaps looser morals looking to make an extra buck. Not that I would know anything about that, personally.

Stella and I tried to cram as many things into her stay as possible. We visited the Smithsonian, George Washington's Mount Vernon Estate, the Mellon Collection at the National Gallery (we fell in love with Vermeer's *Girl in the Red Hat*), the Lincoln Memorial (where Abe looked vaguely like a Roman Emperor ready to don a toga), had beer and French fries at the Alexandria Marina, and spent a night bar hopping in Georgetown.

When Dora arrived by Greyhound bus from New York, I knew it was over. Her roommate was eager to get back to California, and my days with Stella concluded in a tearful goodbye. Stella took the magic with her, and I knew right then and there I needed her back, and not just for another visit, but for all time. A hole had been poked in my heart by her absence.

The brief time in Stella's presence seemed to have mellowed Al somewhat. He removed Pope Paul VI's photo and replaced it with - of all people - John Lennon.

"He's for peace," Al simply said.

I wondered if Al had ever read about Lennon's much debated quote that the Beatles were more popular than Jesus Christ, and John had said he wasn't sure which would be the first to go: rock 'n' roll or Christianity. Anyway, at the crux of it, Lennon was against the Vietnam War, as we all were. On occasion, Al started hanging out with me at the Royal, to nurse one beer to my four or five.

"Don't you get drunk?" he asked.

"Al, it's 3.2 beer. You fill up way before you get drunk. What do you think is the first thing I'm going to do when we get home?"

"Pee?!"

14. CIVIL UNREST

As I came out of the latrine, Major Trammel stopped me. "DeWalt, are you banging Sgt. Evans?"

"Sir?"

"It's a straightforward question, soldier. Yes or no?"

"No, sir."

He grinned. "That means you are. You deny it because you're doing her. If you weren't banging Evans, you'd say you were to let me think so."

Was this some kind of Catch-22 situation? "Sir, I'm not involved with Sgt. Evans in any way. I happen to have a steady girlfriend."

His eyebrows shot up, "Really? And where might she be?"

"In California."

He patted my back, and lowered his voice. "Look, nothing wrong with getting side action. It's every red-blooded soldier's duty to do just that. Congratulations. Evans is quite the package. I'm proud of you."

I couldn't think of anything to say to make the major not proud of me, and returned to my desk. I punned to myself: *this was my first major conversation with the Major.* Minutes later, Lt. Colonel Barone approached, and as I started to get up, he flagged me down. "As you were, DeWalt." He placed three photo headshots on my table. "Recognize him?"

"Yes, sir." He was on General Warner's staff at the Pentagon, who, when not involved in official business, spent time flirting with Lorrie. "It's Colonel Dolan."

"Correct. Dolan's retiring in three weeks. Hence, I'd like you to make him an oversized goodbye card that I can get all his cronies to sign. But I don't want it in pen and black ink linework. I want it in color. Can you do that?"

"I'll need a full complement of narrow and broad-tip color marking pens."

He gave me a look. "What kind?"

"Staedtler Mars, sir."

"You'll have them by thirteen hundred tomorrow."

That's the way it went in the army. Know the right person, and things got accomplished. Otherwise, it was spin your wheels with the usual 'hurry up and wait' bullshit.

Next day, on the dot at thirteen hundred, Schleyer approached, looking none too happy. "A delivery for you." A tag on top read: FOR SPEC-4 DeWalt ONLY. He waited for me to open it. It was a glossy black cardboard box with a sealed flip top lid which I slowly sliced open with surgical precision using an X-ACTO blade, drawing out the moment to agitate Schleyer. His eyes bulged at my assortment of marking pens. "Holy shit! Those are all for you?!"

"Yep. for me, indeed." Schleyer was in charge of Art&Design, but it was now clear, not of me.

Colonel Dolan was an easy cartoonist's target. He was nearly bald, wore oversized Mr.Magoo black-rimmed glasses, and with a perpetual smile, looked a bit like Ike. I drew him sitting on the edge of Lorrie's desk, who had one button of her tight white blouse undone, revealing just a tad of cleavage. An open, pink box filled with colorful donuts sat tantalizingly between them, as Col. Dolan's hand was held aloft. His caption read: *Should I, or shouldn't I?* The inside sentiment as suggested by Barone stated: *To Colonel George Dolan, kudos for your many years of honorable and exemplary service. We wish you the best of luck in civilian life.*

When Barone saw my card, he actually laughed out loud, something I'd never heard him do, or thought he was capable of. "His wife, Agnes, will hate this card, but he'll love it. He's always had a hard-on for Lorri. Great work, DeWalt."

By now, my job had become standard procedure. Other than my cartooning gig, I delivered paperwork to the Pentagon and some surrounding military installations twice a day, at ten-hundred and again at fifteen hundred. Once weekly on Thursday, I chauffeured Colonel Sullivan to his meeting with Major General Warner. No one tracked my movements, and I took time during trips to browse museums and art galleries, and drew in my sketchbook. I had special Army license plates and could park anywhere, other than a red zone, and never stuck a coin into a meter. Since I didn't have a personal car, I ran whatever errands I needed to do while driving the staff vehicle. I took my uniforms to the dry cleaners, got postage stamps, and bought pistachios at a little food specialty shop I'd discovered with Stella in Georgetown.

One morning, Lt. Trent came back into A&D, not to deliver the mail, but to deliver a message. "Listen up troops. You have until next Friday to secure a telephone at your residence. Also, I'll need your number logged in at my office for emergency purposes."

Al and I did not have a phone, nor did most of the men due to the added expense. There were plenty of convenient, if ill kept, public phone booths around town.

"What emergency might that be?" Schleyer asked.

Lt. Trent took his time answering. "Well...there's been lots of civil unrest across the country. Anti-war protestors, peaceniks, hippies, call them what you want, are all growing in size. En masse, they surrounded the Pentagon the other day, right DeWalt?"

"Correct. Colonel Sullivan wasn't too happy about it."

"What the hell was the purpose in surrounding the Pentagon?" Tweed asked.

It was hard to say with a straight face. "They wanted to levitate the building." And as I expected, everyone laughed.

"Be that as it may," Trent said, "if any occurrence takes place at our base after hours, I'd need to call you, not just A&D, but everyone in the unit to gather in force."

"In force? What the hell does that mean?" Mansker asked.

"You will be issued an M-1, plus a regulation steel helmet with liner, and you will arrive in fatigues and combat boots. Everyone here qualifies yearly at the rifle range, so an M-1 should be no stranger to you."

"Wait, hold on," Mansker said. "Then what?"

"In formation, we'll guard the front gate if there's any attempt by protestors to enter the base."

"How about bayonets? Will you issue those?" Mansker said sarcastically.

Trent ignored him.

"And if they try to enter, we...what, shoot them?" Tweed said in a mocking tone. "I'm pretty sure that every person in A&D opposes the damn war in Nam and, most likely, agrees with the protestors, levitating the Pentagon notwithstanding."

"Look, Tweed, I can't discuss personal political beliefs with you. But if the time comes, and I phone, you better get your ass down here ASAP. Got it?"

"Of course. We are duty-bound."

"Fine, that is all."

I found the exchange to be mildly amusing in a time-warp sort of way, like we'd been discussing the arrival of the Visigoths storming the fortress' gate.

15. MAGICAL GIFT

Having a phone gave me the opportunity to call Stella in the privacy from my apartment, instead of hanging onto an abused receiver in a smelly booth where, for some reason, the telephone book was always ripped out. I couldn't help myself and blurted, "Stella, I want you to come back."

"Garrett, I can't leave my new job and take three weeks off to drive cross country, and spend a week with you as much as I would love to, you know that."

"That's not what I'm saying."

"Darling, what are you saying?"

"To stay here, permanently." When I said that, I was thinking for Stella to live with me, like so many people our age were now doing. Upstairs in his attic apartment, Tweed's waitress, Cindy Lou, had moved in.

"You mean to get married?"

At that particular moment, it had not crossed my mind, but by the tone of her voice, I ventured if we were to permanently share a bed, it would be as man and wife. "Yes, that's exactly what I meant. Will you marry me?"

"Are you on bended knee?

"Yes. Of course," I said, doing exactly just that.

"Then, I accept."

Al walked by, took a look and said, "Praying, are we?"

"No, proposing."

"I already said yes," Stella laughed.

"I was talking to Al. Anyway, I'll apply for ten days leave and call back when I can fly out. Can you arrange...the wedding?"

"Umm, sure, why not."

It turned out to be a Lutheran wedding at a small church Stella had on occasion attended. Afterward the brief ceremony, Stella whispered, "You should tip the pastor."

I gave him fifteen dollars in the rectory as he filled out our marriage license. He misspelled my first name by only including one "r" in Garrett. When I pointed it out, he scribbled in the missing "r," making it look like a very obvious and unaesthetic afterthought. Maybe it was the scant tip.

"That's what you get for fifteen bucks," Stella smiled as if I needed to be reminded. We climbed into her VW Bug, ready to make its third cross country trip. In a restaurant somewhere near the Grand Canyon, an older couple kept staring at us. Finally, the man in a cowboy hat came over.

"Don't mean to disturb. But you have the look of happy newlyweds. I just paid for your breakfast. Hope you don't mind."

"Not at all," Stella said. "But if I'd known, I would've ordered the pan-fried steak instead of flapjacks."

"Too late," he grinned.

"Thank you very much," I said. "Much appreciated."

"Good luck to you both."

As we traveled East and northerly, it started getting colder, and when we hit Virginia, it was snowing. Passing through Alexandria to my, or our place, we heard the term "blizzard" on the radio. I'd originally arrived in Alexandria in June, and never even thought that it would snow. Wasn't this the South? People flew Dixie flags, had them painted on their new Camaro car hoods.

I was still in the same Thompson Building, but had left Al for a one-bedroom below street level, a kind of subterranean flat that faced a long unkempt backyard of bamboo and tall grass gone to seed. Now, the grass was no longer visible, covered with deep snow. It was a struggle trudging through it to carry our belongings to the front door. Inside the apartment, Stella shivered, and she's from Minneapolis.

"Oh, my god! It's like an ice box in here. Turn on the heat."

I hadn't warned her. "There is none."

She spun around. "What?"

Mine was the only apartment in the building without radiators, and I imagined Al upstairs reading a book, cozy and warm. The upside was that lacking any heating made the apartment the cheapest in the building.

"But," I said, "we do have a fireplace." I'd stocked up before I left, thinking it would get colder, but not be greeted by a damn blizzard. I had a mess of scrap lumber from our unit dumpster that the carpenters regularly tossed. I got on my knees, balled up a bunch of newspapers, topped it with kindling, and added bigger pieces on top. Once ablaze, we relaxed, but the bed was in the next room over and unfortunately none of the heat carried that far.

Firsts in a new relationship are always magical, like our first time together in our very own apartment; however, that bit of magic was tempered by near freezing toes and hands. We slept in sweats and covered ourselves with every blanket I could find.

That Thursday, on the trip to the Pentagon, Colonel Sullivan asked, "Did you enjoy your stay in California?"

"Yes, sir. I got married."

"I'm sorry?!" he nearly choked. "Married, you said?" He leaned forward and placed his gloved hands on the back of my seat. "Is she expecting?"

Believe it or not, I wasn't familiar with that turn of phrase. I must have missed the *I Love Lucy* episode where censors wouldn't allow the word *pregnant* to be spoken on air, and *expecting* became the final word. And this from a couple that famously slept in separate beds divided by a night stand. I always wondered, who crept into whose bed.

"Expecting what, sir?"

"Is the girl *pregnant*?" he said with emphasis.

"No, sir, Stella is not expecting."

He eased back. "Well, that's good news. You got married on your own volition. How long have you known Stella?"

"About a year, we met in a college art class."

"That's nice. You'll have to bring Stella in."

That sounded ominous. "Bring her in, Sir?"

"Yes. To the photo lab for her picture ID. She's a military dependent and will enjoy all privileges on base as any soldier. Stella will be able to shop at the PX, the commissary — one of the finest in the state — and eat at the cafeteria if she wishes."

"I'll bring her in the first thing tomorrow. Thank you, Sir."

Later in the day as Martin Noble came to collect my weekly cartoon, I mentioned getting married, having an apartment without radiator heating, and how we did our best to soak up every bit of warmth from our raging wood burning fireplace before heading to bed in our sweats.

"Not very conducive to enjoying intimate marital bliss."

"No, it is not."

Two days later, Noble came knocking at our door. "I bear a gift for the newlyweds. Nice to see you again, Mrs. DeWalt." He'd met her earlier at the unit, when she came in for her photo.

She kissed his cheek, eyes bright. "And what do you have for us?"

"It's literally a housewarming gift. Open it."

"Oh, my. An electric blanket!"

To this day, we are eternally grateful to Martin Noble for his magical gift.

16. APPLE CIDER

S tella caused quite a stir when she had arrived in the front lobby. I escorted her inside and Colonel Sullivan's secretary practically upset her chair coming over to greet her. All front office personnel stopped typing or filing to check her out.

"My, she's a tall girl," Mary gushed.

It was somewhat of an ironic comment from Mary who was easily five foot nine herself, but Stella had worn a pair of boots adding a couple of inches to her natural height. Tucked into those boots was a form fitting pair of ski pants, and on top, she had on a bomber jacket with a furry collar. Everyone stared at her as if she was some kind of fashion icon transplant from California.

I beamed with pride. "Mary, I'd like you to meet my wife, Stella."

"A pleasure to meet you." She formally shook Stella's hand and turned to me. "Does that seem strange to you, saying *wife*?"

"Actually, I'm already used to it." I'd said it in my mind many times over during my flight back to get married, and it sounded perfect.

"Okay then. Take Stella to the photo lab, and when you're done, dear, please come back and see Sgt. Evans."

"I have paperwork for you to fill out," she smiled, standing up to offer her hand. Just then, Major Trammel came out of his office and saw Stella and Evans shaking hands. He shook his head as if to say: *Oh, man, DeWalt, you two-timer, now you're really in for it.*

When Harry Mansker heard about my new marital status, he said, "Welcome to the club, buddy. Now you no longer have to pick up those skanky waitresses at the Royal."

"Hey, I resent that!" Tweed said.

"There's skanky waitresses at the Royal?" Herbie Berger said, the guy who arrived the same day I did, but got an official position. At first, it bothered me. Why him and not me? But now, I was happy with the way it turned out, rickety corner table or not.

"I hear they charge five bucks a pop. Right, Tweed?"

"Fuck you, Mansker."

Schleyer came in and looked around. "Okay guys, let's at least pretend to be working."

"Is that all you came back here to tell us?" Mansker said.

"Actually not. The Pentagon is sponsoring an art exhibition to be held on the Concourse. Everyone is invited to submit two works, none larger than three by three feet. I'll post this handout so you can read the details. Oh, no political stuff, or nudity."

"Oh, shoot, I was going to paint my wife, Dena, holding a peace sign while au naturelle," Harry quipped.

"Well, we'll just have to leave that to our imagination," Schleyer said.

Not mine, however.

The idea of being in an art exhibition focused my attention to making an actual painting or two, instead of my usual cartoons or sketchbook pen drawings of Old Town facades. Tweed had recently bought a set of acrylics, a new medium he wanted to try out, but he hated them compared to his oil paints.

"They're too squishy, don't have the right body texture, opacity, or smell right."

I never got the infatuation with artists that use oil paint, who actually like the smell. What I like about acrylics is the *lack* of smell.

I gladly accepted his acrylics, not being a purest about painting in oils like Tweed. Besides my usual load of scrap lumber taken out of the dumpster, I salvaged a piece of Masonite and had a carpenter cut it into two pieces to fit the dimensions required for the Pentagon exhibition. I scavenged some left-over white paint for primer and didn't bother buying canvas, because the Masonite would work just fine.

I waited on the loading ramp for Stella to arrive so I could toss the wood and Masonite pieces into the back seat. Just as Stella pulled up, Lt. Trent walked by.

He tipped his cap at her. "Ah, your wife, is she a woman of leisure?"

"No, she works in display at the new Sears."

He inspected my haul and poked his toe at the wood. "What's this all about?"

"It's for our fireplace."

"Wow, lucky you. You must live in a nice place to have that amenity."

Little did he know, other than Noble's gifted electric blanket, that it was our only source of heat, not some fancy wood burning "amenity." The building was built pre-Civil War. Our subterranean flat had originally been the maid's quarters who used the oversized fireplace to cook in. There was a metal flange attached to the back firewall that swiveled outward with a hook that, presumably, pots were hung from. Stella came up with a brilliant idea and wired a mesh contraption from it to pop popcorn.

We invited Martin Noble over to share in our popcorn, and he brought a gallon jug of apple cider. "It's not to drink...now," he said. He told us it was unpasteurized, bought from a roadside stand, and we needed to add a spoonful of yeast, then cover the open top with a piece of cheesecloth to "let it breathe." In about ten days or so, the concoction would turn into "knock your socks off hard cider." He instructed us to store it in a dry, dark spot, and to gently shake it at least once a day.

"When it's ready, strain it through a new cheesecloth into a clean glass container, drink it, and let the magic begin!"

17. A MASON

My first painting was a portrait of Stella, done mostly with a palette knife in impasto. I like the way acrylics dried quickly, and I could build up texture. The second piece was a still life I set up using our gallon jug of hard apple cider and two tin mugs, one red and the other blue, arranged on a checkered tablecloth. For background, I pinned a poster of folk singer Pete Seeger that I'd removed from a telephone pole. Shot from below, it showed Seeger mouth agape, strumming his banjo, and most likely singing *We Shall Overcome*, a kind of rallying cry against all that was wrong in American society. The gallon jug covered most of his name printed in capital block letters on the bottom of the poster, only making **PE GER** visible. Viewers would get who he was, or not.

When I brought the painting in, Tweed quickly got it. "You do know that Seeger is a political activist and an anti-war proponent."

"Of course."

"And that he's written a song disparaging LBJ."

"Who hasn't done that?" I joked.

But Tweed remained serious. "And you know that some have labeled him a communist, and he was once blacklisted from appearing on TV for ten years."

"Sure, knew that." I did not.

"Hope you don't get any flak over this." He paused to examine my other small painting. "The portrait of Stella looks just like her. Nice job."

Schleyer made a walk-through inspection of our work and offered no opinion. Later in the afternoon, two carpenters came in, bundled up the art, and loaded it into a van to deliver and install at the Pentagon.

Minutes later, Barone approached, again waving me down to remain seated. "This might be a challenge for you." He gave me a head shot of Victor Fiore, a civilian in our unit I barely knew other than getting a nod from him passing through the front lobby with a steel Thermos of coffee. Civilians working for the Army were given GS (Government Schedule) ratings, which had an equivalency to military ranks. The ratings went from GS1 through GS15, with the addition of "supergrades" GS16 through GS18.

Barone explained this to me and said, "Fiore is a GS16, and technically, more or less, equal to the Colonel."

Which explained why Sullivan avoided Fiore at all costs. When they happened into the same room, Sullivan hardly said a word, and it was pretty plain to see that the Colonel disliked his civilian counterpart. It was the old cliché of two chefs in the kitchen make friction.

"The good news, Fiore is retiring," Barone said.

And now, I was supposed to make a funny lighthearted cartoon about a man that the top brass disdained, as did most other NCO's I'd heard from.

"Exactly what is Mr. Fiore's position at the unit, sir?"

"He has a degree in electrical engineering and inspects for approval our exhibit plans that get built into our eighteen wheelers." He gave another look at Fiore's headshot. "Oh, if it's any help, he's a Mason. Good luck."

For the first time, I was stumped. Not only that, what I knew about the Masons could be inscribed onto the cap of my marking pen. *Didn't they have a secret handshake?* I wondered as I went over to ask Tweed. He always seemed to know just enough about something to be informative.

"Masons? Oh, boy, that's a can of worms. Why do you want to know about them?"

"I'm doing a retirement card for Fiore. Barone tells me he's a Mason."

Tweed sat back and crossed his arms over his chest. "I'm half surprised that, in the past, Colonel Sullivan and Fiore haven't come to blows. In a nutshell, the Nazis hated Masons, as did the Communists and the Catholic church. Jesse in Supply, he could never be a Mason."

"Why?"

"He's black. Nor could your lovely wife."

"Because she's a Lutheran?"

"No," he chuckled, "they don't allow women. A lot of GS employees join the Masons as a way of making connections and getting the inside scoop on promotions. It's a fraternal order and they help each other rise through the ranks."

"Thanks for the info." It didn't help me one bit in formulating any cartoon potential for the man. Physically, he had perfectly trimmed Pomaded black hair, sported a Clark Gable mustache, had knife-edge creased dark slacks, and always wore crisp starched long-sleeved white shirts with a silk regimental tie.

Over dinner at home, I told Stella about being stumped of any idea regarding doing Fiore's retirement card.

"Just play it straight," she said. "Don't make an attempt to be funny, draw the man for what he is."

The problem was: *what was he?*

18. OUT OF CONTENTION

I followed Stella's suggestion, and drew him standing by a drafting desk spilling over with blueprints which, I imagined, was his job to read and check for errors. In one hand, he held a metal square, and in the other, an oversized compass. Together, they formed the Mason's fraternal symbol. On his tie, I put the letter G, also part of Masonic symbology, which either stood for Geometry or God, depending on whom you asked.

The front caption read: CONGRATULATIONS ON BECOMING A CIVILIAN! Then on the inside, I wrote: OOPS! YOU ALREADY WERE ONE.

It wasn't brilliant, but it was the best I could come up with.

"Not bad, not bad at all," Barone said when I showed it to him. He leaned in. "And good riddance to you Fiore, I feel like adding. But I won't. Must observe convention, right, DeWalt?"

"Of course, sir." I left for the Pentagon, to take in my first viewing of our Art&Design Concourse exhibit. It was kind of a magical feeling seeing my two pieces, with all the others, displayed in a cement fortress that was the center representing all of the American military branches, or as was said, "Ground Zero."

A well-dressed woman in heels, in her early forties sidled up. "What's this?"

I thought it pretty obvious. "An art exhibit."

"Done by civilians?"

"No, ma'am, by men in uniform, the Army to be specific."

"That's funny. I've seen art exhibits by the Navy and it's all about their magnificent ships, or the Air Force with their jets streaming through the sky. But where are the Army battle scenes or depictions of soldiers? This looks like something I'd see at a downtown Georgetown gallery, nothing military about it."

How could I explain we really were nothing more than a bunch of civilians thrown together at the Exhibit Unit, who played soldiers in uniforms weekly from eight to five (or from oh-eight hundred to seventeen hundred) and did our best to serve out our stay with a minimum of hassle?

"Is this what taxpayers are funding, for soldiers to paint still lifes, portraits, and scenics while on duty?"

"All of these paintings were done on our time, weekends and after hours."

"Ah...really? I take it you might be in this show?"

I pointed to one of my two pieces. "That's my wife."

She popped on a pair of reading glasses and got close. "I like her hair; how does she get it that way?"

"Hairspray."

"Of course. Well then, carry on and keep painting." She started to walk off, turned back and poked my chest with a well-manicured fingernail. "...on your spare time."

"Yes. ma'am." I assumed she was a mid-level GS, possibly working as a bursar or in some accounting division. I left the Concourse and headed for General Warner's office to make my one delivery.

"Just made a fresh pot," Lorri chirped as I entered. Not only that, there was always a nice arrangement of ceramic mugs, no Styrofoam for her or the general's staff.

"I've got paperwork for the General that requires his signature."

"Fine. Walk it on back."

"Me?"

"Yes, to his inner sanctum." She filled her mug. "He won't bite your head off."

I had never come face to face with Major General Keith Warner, and had only seen him at a distance in the conference room when I came to retrieve Colonel Sullivan. The General had quite the reputation as a World War II warrior fighting Nazis, having earned the Medal of Honor. He was also a personal friend of the highly decorated combat veteran, Audie Murphy. "Do I salute and stand at attention?"

"Only if he requests your presence, and you are reporting to him. This is different. You need not stand at attention, but don't slouch either."

"Are you saying, I slouch?"

"Get outta here. Make your delivery."

I walked through the first large space, the conference room which had a polished boat shaped table surrounded by fourteen leather executive swivel chairs. Six to a side and one at each end. On the wall was a framed black and white photo of the current Chief-of-Staff, and one of President Lyndon Johnson. I continued into his suite, where the general was lighting up possibly the largest cigar I'd ever seen. Behind him was a glass-fronted trophy case with various plaques and photos that mostly seemed from the World War II era, and one distinctive German Luger. Ironically, I could see no photos or memorabilia making reference to Vietnam.

"Morning, General. A delivery from Colonel Sullivan." I handed him the brown clasp envelope.

"Ah, yes, you're Sully's driver."

"Yes, sir." Sully? I guess if you're a general you can call a full-bird colonel by nickname.

He blew smoke at the ceiling. "How's he treating his men?"

I thought it out of place as a Spec-4 to pass judgment on my ultimate superior officer, but I had to offer something. "Colonel Sullivan is...ah, a terrific CO, on all accounts, sir."

Warner nodded, but didn't reply. He pulled open a drawer from his large oak desk, propped up his feet on top, and tilted back in his chair. "Give me a sec to read this," he said, motioning me with his cigar to take a seat. A few minutes later, I heard Lorri's voice come over his squawk box.

"Barry's here. Have time for him?"

"Sure, send him back."

Barry? Barry Goldwater the senator? Was there another important Barry that wanted to see General Warner? Turned out to be a staff sergeant by the name of Barry Sadler, with a guitar slung over his shoulder. I recognized him from his *Ballads of the Green Berets* LP album cover in the Concourse bookstore, where I opted instead to buy *Rubber Soul* by the Beatles.

"Hey, Barry," General Warner said, "meet Specialist DeWalt, he's at Cameron Station with the Exhibit Unit."

"The what?"

"Doesn't matter."

We shook hands, and Warner handed me the signed paperwork which I stuffed back in the envelope. "Nice meeting you, Sergeant."

"Yeah...sure, likewise."

Lorri blocked the doorway as I started to leave her office. "You got married and didn't tell me."

"How do you know?"

"You fart at the Exhibit Unit, and an hour later I'll know about it."

"Interesting metaphor."

"I guess that takes you out of contention."

"I had no idea I was ever in...contention."

"You do know Washington DC statistics, don't you?"

"Regarding what, exactly?"

"There are four women for every man in the City, therefore you were in contention." She stepped aside and blew me a kiss as I left. Outside in the corridor, two field grade officers were having a discussion. I slowed to partially overhear.

"...we have the mightiest military forces in the world, Marines, Navy, Air Force, and Army. How the fuck are a bunch of peasants in black pajamas with nothing more than a damn rice bag slung over their shoulder to feed themselves, gonna beat us in Nam?"

"You're right. No fucking way. Eighteen more months and we clean the whole goddamn mess up. Guaranteed."

I lingered, pretending to read my envelope.

"But you know, that South Vietnamese leadership is pretty fucked up and corrupt. Sometimes I wonder why we bother to prop them up."

"Anything's better than Communism. Right?"

The other officer didn't answer.

19. CIRCLE OF FRIENDS

"Barry Sadler?" Stella asked. "I hear his song about the Green Berets on the radio all the time. But once is plenty, I switch stations. What was he like?"

"Ordinary guy, except he has a best-selling album, is in the Army, struts around the Pentagon with his guitar, and seems to have easy access to General Warner."

Our phone rang, and I crossed my fingers that it wasn't Lt. Trent requesting that I show up on base ASAP to be issued an M1 plus bayonet to march lockstep with my other brothers in arms to quell a potential breaching of the gates by a horde of war protesting peaceniks. Actually, I was on their side, but in uniform, I didn't have much choice but to follow orders.

The phone call turned out to be from Martin Noble.

"How's that cider coming along?" he asked.

"Fine. A bit cloudy around the edges. Hey, come on over and let's sample it."

"That's exactly what I was hoping y'all would say. You mind if I bring a friend?"

"Not at all." I was going to ad: *bring her*, but didn't due to Stella's previous suspicions, which were corroborated when Martin walked in with a male friend.

"Garrett, Stella, this is Tom, he works over in Georgetown at the International Safeway in the deli section."

Tom had blond hair almost to his collar and wore a tight black T-shirt with a white dove holding an olive branch in its beak. END

WAR was printed below. That, plus his faded jeans and perfectly white low-cut tennies minus socks, meant he would never be mistaken for a GI in civilian clothes. Martin had brought a large carafe, and decanted the cider through a fresh piece of cheesecloth he'd been smart enough to bring, since we had none. The bottom of the gallon jug had residue and we tossed it into the trash.

"Cute place you have here," Tom said.

Of all the words to use and describe our subterranean flat, "cute" would be on the bottom of my list. Impoverished, second-hand, abused, and unheated kind of came to mind, but perhaps I was being somewhat overly harsh. Stella had done her best within our limited budget to make it homey. At a local second hand store, she'd bought an oval braided rug for the front of the fireplace. On sale at Sears, she'd picked up a lightweight paisley cover to throw over our daybed, a terrific place when the fire roared. Once, I'd made the fire so hot that the varnish on a nearby wooden chair started smoking. A couple of days later when we were short of wood, I tossed the chair in.

She'd also bought a colorful, folk-art style ceramic rooster for no other reason than she liked looking at it, which held a prominent place in our near empty bookcase.

I took out a kitchen match, struck it, and lit the fire.

"Wow, that is one huge fireplace, never seen anything like it. You could roast a pig in there," Tom exclaimed.

"I think, at one time, they did," Stella said.

"Frank Lloyd Wright said that the hearth is the heart of a home," Tom noted.

"Well, it is for us, plus a certain electrical blanket."

"But if the fireplace is your only source of heat, what do you do in the morning when you get up?" Tom asked.

"I go into the kitchen and turn on all four stove burners."

Tom moaned. "Stella, no, you'll asphyxiate yourself!"

Stella laughed. "We're still here aren't we. Realistically though, this whole apartment is as airtight as a sieve."

I'd pinned up several of my watercolors which were Cubist-inspired cityscapes of buildings I'd done around our Old Town neighborhood.

"Is that your art?" Tom asked.

"Yes. But at the unit, thanks to Martin, I'm the official Exhibiteer newsletter cartoonist. And I'm a company driver for our CO, and-"

"Enough shop talk," Martin cut me off. "Stella, if you please, I need four drinking implements so we can sample this homemade hard cider."

Opinions varied with Martin as the number one supporter. Tom thought it was "pretty good" and Stella said she could "take or leave it." My take, "I prefer beer."

We sat on the floor on the braided rug in front of our blazing fireplace, warming up considerably, with a three-foot snow drift surrounding the building. There was a knock on the door, and Martin joked, "Oh, oh, probably the ABC ready to bust our asses for drinking illegal hooch!"

I answered the door and invited Al in, holding a Time magazine.

"Well hello, Father Vicente. How goes it, Padre?" Martin said, face now visibly flushed. Almost everyone at the unit knew that Al was still seriously contemplating joining the priesthood.

He handed me the Time. "There's an article about a new museum opening in New York called the Whitney. I know you like contemporary art and I thought you'd be interested in reading about it."

"Thank you. Come and join us."

"Al, taste this fine home-made hard apple cider," Martin said.

"Thanks, I'll pass."

"Al, one sip won't hurt. Priests can drink. Right, Tom?"

"I'm pretty sure."

"You'll still make it into heaven. St. Peter won't bar you at the Pearly Gates, or...me, I guess. I'm a Baptist in good standing. Or do they only allow in Catholics?"

"You'll find out, Martin," Al said, sitting down in our one wing back chair, eyeing our scene with caution.

I went into the kitchen to get a beer for Al, because I was confident he'd nurse one to be sociable. As I stood there momentarily, refrigerator door ajar, a thought struck me. There were three guys surrounding Stella, and not one would even attempt to flirt with her. Martin had brought his boyfriend Tom, and Al, for all I knew, was celibate. This was my current circle of friends.

20. PHOTO OPPORTUNITY

Looking back on it now, it's hard to believe, but Stella and I broke into the Pentagon. Actually, we didn't exactly break in, but we did sneak in. Even though I went there on a daily basis, I was never told that one needed a pass to enter the building after eighteen-hundred. Stella had picked me up at the unit after work, and I took the driver's wheel to head up to the Pentagon to show her the A&D art exhibit.

I parked in the civilian section of the lot where I usually put the staff car, and we went up the granite steps to be halted by an MP.

"Pass?" he said.

"Pass for what?"

"To enter the building after office hours."

"But I'm in uniform," I protested.

"Doesn't matter. I repeat, you need a pass!"

It was kind of odd to consider the Pentagon as an office building, but that's what it was with slightly over 25,000 employees that came in two morning shifts, so as not to cause parking gridlock. I grabbed Stella's hand. "Let's go, I have an idea."

I drove around to the other side where I'd seen buses and taxis drop off people in a kind of semi-underground parking structure. Now, both civilians and military were streaming out of the building, everybody most likely happy to get the hell out of this giant cement superstructure to rush home for their liquor cabinet.

"Right there," I said.

"What?"

"The stairwell with the white metal door at the top. We're taking it."

She scanned the emerging crowd anxiously. "For real? How about the MPs?"

"See any?" I was in uniform, and Stella was nicely dressed in her work clothes, panty hose and all. We would not look out of place. This wasn't two rogue hippies in bell bottoms and tie-dyed T-shirts shouldering protest signs to invade the Pentagon. At the top of the stairwell, I held my breath as I grabbed the door knob. It opened, and the next thing we knew, both of us were casually strolling the Concourse. She loved seeing her portrait and the other artistic efforts from my Army colleagues. Al had lately become fascinated with tropical birds, and painted toucans, parrots, macaws, and quetzals, done in my former bedroom now turned into his full-blown art studio.

I wondered if there was a subconscious push-back on Al's part by depicting the hyper color of the bird's plumage in contrast that he might be wearing a black suit and white collar for life.

We left the Concourse and spent most of the time giggling on the drive home, repeatedly chanting, "We snuck into the Pentagon!" We'd performed a bit of magic in a building that certainly had its occult connections due to its shape...the five-sided pentagon, or pentagram, was said to be a satanic symbol that personified self-gratification and personal power. Maybe, that assessment wasn't too far off.

At home, nestled on our daybed, each reading a book as our fire was in mid-burn, Stella asked, "Do you have any more vacation time left this year?"

"I'll check with Mary tomorrow."

Following day, I asked Mary what the status of my leave-taking was. She pulled a binder off a shelf, and thumbed through it. "Twelve days. Planning a trip?"

"Working on it. Thanks."

"Oh, don't go anywhere." Mary waved Brian Selzer over, one of our unit photographers, as he stood by the coffee urn, big camera in hand. She then opened a packet with my name on it, handing me a Spec-5 patch. "A higher rank," she smiled warmly, clicking on her squawk box. "Colonel, DeWalt and Selzer are here."

"Fine, send them in."

Inside his office I stood shoulder to shoulder with Colonel Sullivan posing with the Spec-5 patch held against my sleeve. In the background was a huge sepia photo mural of a forward charging tank. Selzer popped off several flash photos as Sullivan said, "Congratulations, m'boy."

I got promoted, and was now of equal rank to Schleyer, head of A&D. The packet contained patches to be attached to the sleeves of my Army Greens, khakis, TWs, fatigues, and my field jacket. When I showed them to Tweed, he chuckled, "Looks like Stella is going to have a lot of sewing to do, unless you know how?"

"Nope." We were supposed to learn in basic, but I never got around to it.

He handed me a pair of scissors and a roll of double-sided sticky tape. "For fun, stick on your new chevrons, then slowly walk past Schleyer's desk. That should royally piss him off."

I did, feeling his dagger glare as I strolled out.

The boost in rank meant more money which would make a twelve-day vacation much easier on our budget.

Stella was elated. "As soon as it's Spring, let's go to Minneapolis. That is a great time to go. Garrett, what do you think?"

"I've always wanted to go to the land of 10,000 lakes."

"Really? Not being sarcastic?"

"Of course not."

That night we had magical sex.

21. FAMOUS PEOPLE

"Sir, if I'm not mistaken, that's John Steinbeck coming down the stairs."

Sullivan removed his reading glasses and looked out of his backseat window. "Indeed, it is." He snapped his attaché case shut. "Well, he's a personal friend of Lyndon Johnson, and has a son stationed in Vietnam." The colonel made no move to exit the staff car as we watched Steinbeck hail a cab. "In a way, I feel the man is being somewhat hypocritical of his own beliefs. Steinbeck's an old leftie, champion of the masses, the dispossessed, a union supporter, not one you'd expect to get all rah-rah about supporting our Vietnam conflict. It seems once his son got drafted, he...well let's say, switched ideology?"

It was a statement I might have expected from an instructor in a college philosophy class, not a high-ranking military officer. Steinbeck had another son who also ended up in the Army, and served in Vietnam. Many decades later in LA, Stella and I would be introduced to one of Steinbeck's sons at an art opening, but I don't remember which one (Thomas or John IV?), and neither does Stella. Possibly, we'd had a lot to drink that night.

Over beer that evening at the Royal, Stella said, "First Barry Sadler, now John Steinbeck. Who the heck could be next?"

Next, turned out to be Omar Bradley, the five-star general of WWII fame, who along with Eisenhower, George Marshall, and MacArthur were the few to achieve the lofty rank. (The very one General LeMay* wanted, but got blackballed by LBJ.) But I'm fudging here, I delivered a message to Bradley's office but never saw him.

"Is the General in today?" I inquired from a captain manning the reception desk.

"Who are you with?" he said, not bothering to look up.

I decided to go one up on Sullivan. "I'm with General Warner's office. This needs to be signed by your CO."

"Yes. Right away." he stood up quickly, and for a second I thought he'd salute me. Then he took a moment to appraise me, and without being asked, volunteered a bit of info. "Technically, General Bradley retired in 1953, but as a general, you could say he is always active in some capacity. Currently, he serves on an advisory board for Lyndon Johnson. So, we staff his office just in case he should choose to come in."

There would be another "next," and he was a "big next" at six foot three. And the man was none other than John Wayne, AKA the Duke. The meeting happened by chance as I accompanied Colonel Sullivan into General Warner's office who was chatting with Wayne, making the general look even shorter than he was.

"Morning fellas," Warner said, "Mr. Wayne's here to make a movie about the Green Berets, and he's going to use SSgt. Sadler's song."

Sullivan shook the movie star's hand, and I nodded, thinking this was one movie I'd be sure to miss.

"By the way, Specialist DeWalt is from your neck of the woods, Duke."

Wayne slowly turned to me. "Newport Beach?"

"Yes, sir." How Warner knew this, I wasn't sure.

"I'll be damned. Where did you go to school?"

"Orange Grove College."

His eyes brightened. "They have the best damn rowing team in the country. I'm a big fan. OGC beats four-year colleges, and they're only a *two-year junior* college."

"Yes, sir." I knew his fandom well. Wayne owned one of those inflatable rubber rafts with a motor strapped on back to cruise the bay. He often pulled alongside the shell, shouting encouragement at the OGC rowing team.

Sullivan politely cleared his throat, signaling for me to take my leave, so he could have his own personal moment with the Duke. I left and Lorri quickly followed me out the office, practically pinning me to the corridor wall.

"You talked to *him*?"

"Yes. We're both from Newport Beach."

"Hmm. Do you think he'd give me an autograph if I asked?"

"Ask him, and find out."

Stella wasn't impressed with Wayne any more than she was with SSgt. Sadler. Evidently, Wayne raised her proto-feminist ire due to his swaggering movie persona.

I mentioned to her that in Basic Training, our DI called anyone who was a showoff, "A fucking John Wayne." It bugged them that Wayne did not pull any military service during the Big One, unlike Jimmy Stewart, Clark Gable, and Kirk Douglas.

One of Sullivan's rules was that when we went out in public, especially at bars, we had to dress in civilian clothes. My warmest outerwear was my field jacket, and for that reason, I didn't have Stella sew on my Spec-5 patches so it would look more civilian, since a lot of young people, ironically, had developed a passion for wearing military gear even though they opposed all things involving the Army.

It had stopped snowing a couple of weeks ago, but I still zipped up my field jacket to pull the draw string tight around my waist as Stella and I walked to the library. She had plenty of warm clothes inherited from her Minneapolis days, plus a pair of thermals. At only seven feet wide, we passed the narrowest house in Old Town and possibly in America. It was two stories tall, and occupied.

"If we parked our VW Bug in front of this house, the car would be longer than the place is wide," Stella said. "Hard to believe someone lives in there."

As a local oddity, Tweed had suggested we have a look at it. He'd said that the space between the two houses was once a narrow alleyway that horse and buggy drivers would scrape through as a shortcut, leaving hub gouges on the exterior walls. Eventually, the owner put a stop to it by bricking it up into a two-story house that he let his butler live in. Because of his alley-blocking measure, neighbors dubbed it the "Spite House."

At the library, I checked out *The Secret of Santa Victoria*, and Stella nabbed *Valley of the Dolls*. When I gave her the stink eye at her choice of reading material, she said, "I know it's trashy, but one of my female coworkers said it's very entertaining and fun. So there."

* *Many years later, General LeMay's wife, Helen, would become a student of mine in a painting class. She invited me to their home, and introduced me to the General who was on his ham radio speaking to Senator Barry Goldwater.*

22. RAISING THE COLORS

Finally, we made a decision to take eleven days off for a trip to Stella's hometown, Minneapolis. According to a Rand McNally map at the library, the distance was 1,115 miles, a seventeen-hour drive. Two days to get there and two to return meant a four-day bite taken out of our vacation just for driving.

To say the least, I was "blown away" by Minneapolis. Unlike downtown LA, which seemed scattered to the four winds, the city's downtown actually makes sense. Tidy, organized, and pedestrian friendly, it even has one main street dedicated to buses and taxis only to ease traffic flow. Across the Mississippi was its twin city, St. Paul, but we didn't visit it for a couple more days. The big landmark downtown was the Art Deco Foshay Tower, the city's tallest building at about five hundred feet. The sides tapered as it went up and was constructed to resemble the Washington Masonic Temple in Alexandria, Virginia, which I thought was a weird coincidence. We traveled from Alexandria to Minneapolis to be greeted by two, near look-alike buildings.

Storefronts at second floor levels had glass enclosed pedestrian bridges called the "Skyway System" that connected one exterior to another across the street.

"In the winter, you really appreciate the system because they are temperature controlled and you can cover lots of shops from one side of town to the other without ever going outside and freezing your butt off," Stella said, with a measure of relief in her voice at the memory of it. She took me to some of her favorite places, including the Nanking, a Chinese restaurant (she showed me how to handle chopsticks), and a little shop that sold caramel corn, her high school snack of choice. We went to a cafe which, with an order of beer, offered free peanuts in the shell. Everyone tossed the shells on the floor and they crunched underfoot as we settled into a window seat behind cafe curtains to watch a parade of pedestrians stream by. One minute, it was smartly dressed office workers with attaché cases, next it could be a group of university students in preppie style clothes, a farmer in bib overalls holding hands with his wife in a gingham dress window shopping, and the occasional small group of long-haired American Indians in Levis, denim shirts, and cowboy boots.

"We have a lot of Indians that live here in the city and State. After all, Minnesota is the Sioux word for 'sky-blue waters,'" Stella said. "And there's always Minnehaha being cradled by Hiawatha."

That eluded me. "Sorry?"

"It's a statue, I'll take you to it later."

After we left the café, I bought a T-shirt with a large mosquito silk-screened on it with the caption: STATE BIRD. The bloodthirsty monsters came out at sundown and nearly sucked me dry, and they did seem big as a bird. Stella's father, Nicholas, laughed and rationalized the skeeters seemed to prefer me, "since you're fresh blood from California." Actually, the loon is the State Bird. Yet I never saw one.

Out of the 10,000 lakes, we went to five and swam in three. The nearest one, Lake Harriet, was two blocks from Stella's house on Lyndale with a pleasant, short hike through an opulent rose garden which we walked through every day. Harriet had convenient swimming spots, a stretch of sandy beach, and grass that edged right up to the water where people spread out their blankets. There was also a dock about twenty yards off-shore were boys lurked to dive from at arriving girls, and cop a free feel underwater. When Stella had once complained to the lifeguard, his reply was typical for the day, "Boys will be boys."

Lake Harriet is three miles around, and years later as the running fad kicked in, would become the perfect practice run for a 10K. Her father fished the lake for crappie, which is not pronounced the way you might think. It's 'croppie.' He pan-fried them in cornmeal and they were delicious.

One of the scariest days of my life would come one morning as Nicholas woke me when it was still dark, and said, "Come with me."

"How about Stella?"

"She's been there, done that," he said.

I got dressed and we took the bus to the City Hall Court House which had a four-faced clock tower that had been the tallest in the city until the Foshay Tower was built. Nicholas mentioned that the faces of the clock were bigger than London's Big Ben. At City Hall, Nicholas worked in maintenance and one of his many jobs was to hoist the American flag from the tower's flagpole. To me, it was a heroic undertaking. He retrieved the flag, and after an elevator ride, it was all steps. Many steps. Eventually, the stairs became an iron spiral in open air we continued up, and I could feel the wind surge around me. This seemed a classical spot for instant onset vertigo. If I lost my balance and fell, I'd most likely break every bone in my body, yet I was following a man with only one working eye. Eventually we reached a platform way too high for my comfort, where Nicholas readied the flag to run up the pole. I've never had a fear of heights, but this was challenging my perception as I looked out across the city skyline, stomach clenched.

"You do this every morning?" I asked.

"And in the evening. Flag doesn't come down by itself."

"What happens when it snows?"

Nicholas looked at me as if the answer was pretty damn obvious. "Then it snows, and I still raise and lower the colors."

Nicholas would do this until the day he retired without ever losing his footing, no matter how inclement the weather. I couldn't wait to get back down to street level.

I took the bus back to Stella's just in time for her mom, Alexi, to start preparing breakfast. Stella was in shorts and a T-shirt, minus a bra, which got her a look from Alexi as I entered until she gave it a second thought and realized I was the husband. Alexi worked part time as a cashier at Red Owl, a grocery chain founded in Minnesota with stores throughout the upper Midwest. She served up scrambled eggs, hash browns, toast, and coffee. Alexi was a pleasant unassuming woman who put pin curls in her hair to make it look "nice." Like her husband, she was not prideful because that would be "tooting your own horn," which was strictly bad manners in Minnesota. When it came to breakfast or lunch, that was always served at the kitchen table. The dining room was for dinner or when guests came over. Conversations were generally about anything that wasn't controversial, political, religious, or something that could stir up passions. The corn crop or weather was always a good topic since it could change on a dime. One minute it was clear blue skies, next minute skies grew dark and leaden, and you got a massive downpour.

"What are you kids up to today?" she asked.

I guess to her we were kids. "Going to the Walker," Stella said.

"Bring jackets, you never know…" she said, removing her apron to sit and eat with us. "Eggs okay?"

"Delish," Stella and I chimed.

"You're not driving to the Walker, are you?" Alexi said, sounding worried.

"Course not, Mom."

The four-door family Dodge was parked in an unattached one-car garage with a dirt floor at the end of the backyard where there was a trellis that supported a crop of cucumbers for future pickling. The Walker Art Center was located at the nucleus of a very busy intersection called Five Points, which Stella refused to drive to.

"One wrong turn and we could end up in Wisconsin, or wherever."

We took the bus, something I never did back home or wanted to.

I fell in love with the Walker at first sight. Just the right size to be enjoyable and not overwhelming like the Louvre. Filled with contemporary art, it shared a large front lobby with the Guthrie Theater where we saw Arthur Miller's devastating play, *The Crucible*. (The existential question that Miller's masterpiece posed was: *Should you lie under oath to save a life?*)

23. CENSER

The home Stella was born and raised in was a two-story white clapboard with a blue asphalt tile roof. It had an extended enclosed front porch the width of the house. There was a full basement and an attic you could live in, which an older sister and her newly married husband once occupied before finding their own place. In a way, it was almost a four-story. Many years later, after Nicholas died, when Alexi hit her eighties, she decided that assisted living for mature adults might be a better bet than remaining in her homestead. There was only one bathroom and it was upstairs. Her aging legs were taking a beating, not to mention general upkeep becoming too much of a chore. She called us and offered it for sale at ten percent below market price for $38,000 which we could afford.

To imagine living in that grand home was a magical moment. It fronted a pleasant two-lane street where oaks and Dutch elms grew over from one side to the other creating a leafy canopy to drive under. I loved that house and, on impulse, was prepared to sell ours, ready to write a check when Stella said, "No."

"No?"

"Two words. SNOW and SNOW."

As much as she also loved the house, she explained the whole maintenance procedure. Window screens had to be taken down in winter and put back on in Spring, the weather was harsh on the wood siding and her dad painted one side per season, meaning every four years he did it again. "Do you want to stand on that tall ladder and reach under the eaves to paint? Dad did it, and it's a miracle he never fell. The sidewalk has to be shoveled clear of snow almost daily. Ready for that? Let's talk cars. Snow tires have to be put on for winter and the oil has to be swapped out for a lighter blend that won't freeze. I could go on…"

"I get the point."

"Did I mention the hurricanes?"

"Okay, stop."

As much as we all had great memories of Grandma's house, Stella phoned her mother that we wouldn't be moving to Minneapolis and were firmly settled into our three-bedroom condo. Alexi asked how much we'd paid. Although I heard Stella say, "$81,000 dollars," I didn't hear what was said on the other end. But I can I imagine what the woman must have thought we were: either crazy, insane, wasteful, naive, or we got conned by a devious real estate agent.

She did tell Stella, "Why on earth would you pay nearly fifty-thousand dollars more for a place half the size of mine? And it doesn't come with a cellar!"

"It's California, Mom."

If that very house could be magically airlifted and plunked down in Newport Beach at that time, the asking price would have been $181,000.

We flew to Minneapolis many times in our ensuing civilian life and always enjoyed the city, lakes, parks, museums, and how the Walker Art Center expanded over the years to include an immense sculpture garden that became the perfect location for Claes Oldenburg's *Spoonbridge With Cherry*. I bought a T-shirt with the image.

I loved the down-home attitude of Stella's family, and during one visit without sounding too confrontational, I said, "Alexi, I have to ask. Everything I've read about Czechoslovakia tells me it's a Catholic nation. So, why are you a Lutheran?"

She was making Stella's favorite dish, chicken dumplings. "Do you know what a censer is?"

"Sure, a guy that bans books or movies,"

She cast me a motherly smile. "That's spelled c e n s o r. This is spelled c e n s e r. It's a thurible."

"A terrible?" I joked, still not having any idea what she was talking about.

"Well, it was *terrible* for me. The censer is a metal ball hung from a chain, filled with burning incense, that the priest swings back and forth, sort of to symbolize prayers rising to heaven. I had an immediate negative reaction to the smoke, almost got sick. I hated it. I was about twelve, attending church with my grandparents and I dashed out. I walked down the street, entered a Lutheran Church, and started attending their services. My grandparents never said a word. To them, one church was as good as another."

"As long as it was Christian," Stella added.

Nicholas was rolling cigarettes outside on the small rear patio. Alexi would not let him smoke in the house (or drive because of the one eye). Before going outside, he asked me what section of the newspaper I wanted. When I said Arts and Entertainment, he cast me a negative shrug as if a guy like me would want Sports.

Just before we went on leave to Minneapolis, Martin Noble wanted to know the name of my hometown paper. "Why?" I asked.

"I'm sending the photo of you posing for your promotion with Colonel Sullivan, plus a small article about you. Local newspapers love that shit. Celebrate the boys in uniform and all that crap."

That article however, would never catch the eyes of my father. He subscribed to the Los Angeles Times Mirror, and dismissed the local paper as a "dumb rag."

"Why would I want to read about some drunk yokel who runs off the road and smashes into an orange tree," he'd rhetorically stated more than once, tearing up another mailer from the local press asking us to subscribe. "I want to read about national and international news, like what's going on with NATO, or in the Suez Canal, or what Kennedy and Khrushchev have up their sleeve."

24. HOME FREE

After I returned from our Army leave and first ever trip to Minneapolis, Mary greeted me in the front lobby and sighed, "We missed you."

"Really?"

"Yes, the substitute driver I picked at random didn't turn out well. His last name should've been an omen. Spec-4 Butts."

I'd met him at a costume party in Noble's apartment where Mike Butts had dressed up by painting a target on his face. "What's with the target?" I asked.

"In grade school, I was the target and butt of many jokes because of my last name," he said without much apparent irony.

"Do tell," Stella remarked.

Butts worked in the model shop and now, according to Mary, Sullivan had banished him to the paint supply shop, possibly the least desirable place in the Exhibit Unit. He'd be wearing a respirator all day, standing in a spray booth with overhead fans roaring away. "Why did he demote and transfer Butts?"

"He showed up late for Sully's Pentagon briefing with General Warner. And as we say, the shit hit the fan. Butts was demoted one rank and fined forty-five dollars. Anyway, welcome back." She got up to get a coffee. "One thing, all accrued days of leave that you choose *not* to take, you'll be paid for when you get out. Think about it, it's like money in the bank."

Stella and I did think about it and we decided to leave nine days "in the bank." Not only that, but both of us were paid ten cents a mile to our point of draft origin. It made me wish I'd been surfing in Hawaii when I was drafted - but then I wouldn't have met Stella. On my last day at the Exhibit Unit, I went into Barone's office to get my discharge papers and officially sign out.

"Stop by Sullivan's office before you leave," he said.

I went around the corner, found the door open, approached his desk, and even though I was in civilian clothes, I saluted nonetheless. "Specialist DeWalt, sir."

He returned the salute and came around his desk to shake my hand. "You did good work, m'boy." He then took a typed letterhead on official Army stationary off his desk. "The establishment you worked at when drafted, Trend Interiors, by law has to rehire you. I'm sending this letter to let them know. Also, there's a letter from General Warner in appreciation of all the cartoon cards you made. Good luck, and give my best to your lovely wife."

"Yes, sir."

Another Army benefit we weren't aware of was that GIs with the rank of E-5 and above would have all their household belongings moved home for free. When the moving van trucker came into our apartment with a younger guy along, he said, "This is all ya got? Hell's bells this could probably fit into a station wagon."

Not a VW Bug, however. We basically had my uniforms, our winter clothes, dishes, kitchenware, a dozen books, a portable record player, and six LPs. But when I pointed to all of my paintings on the wall, he changed his tune.

"Seventeen," he counted slowly. "Okay, that takes up more space. How about the braided rug?"

Stella looked at all the burn holes from our fireplace sparks. "Nah, leave it for the next couple to enjoy."

I started to remove my biggest canvas from the wall, a full-length portrait of Stella reading a book in a wingback chair.

"Hold it! Please don't touch anything. For insurance purposes we wrap and box everything. If something gets damaged, it's our fault not yours."

Only one item broke. Stella's colorful ceramic rooster.

As much as I shuddered at the thought of spending two years in uniform (and possibly ending up in Nam), plus anticipating all the regulations and inspections that came with it, our stay in Alexandria, Virginia, was pretty much a magical time. It was an eight to five job with weekends off. There were plenty of firsts; the first Christmas which we celebrated by decorating our scraggly tree with empty Budweiser beer cans, the first homemade hard cider, first drink of moonshine offered by an old lady that ran a small deli around the corner (it tasted like kerosene spiked with sake), our first dance at Martin's costume party, and our First Anniversary celebrated at a Potomac dockside restaurant where we ordered another first: frog legs. Tastes like chicken.

And not to forget perhaps the most memorable, we did sneak into Fortress Pentagon.

At the Smithsonian, we saw the Star-Spangled Banner and the Wright brothers' Kitty Hawk plane.

Then, there were all the great works from artists that we viewed in museums: Jasper Johns, Robert Motherwell, Picasso, Gaugin, Rothko, and Stella's personal favorite work, Renoir's enchanting *Luncheon of the Boating Party* at the Phillips Collection. We had a great time together, and, in a nutshell, the two years had been magical.

25. DEAD GOPHERS

Back in California, we found a one-bedroom upper floor apartment in Costa Mesa on Harbor Blvd., one of Orange County's longest streets, that does not end up at any harbor. But it gets you within a couple of miles of Newport Beach. Stella was not guaranteed her old job back by law, as I was. She found a position at the Pennysaver, in the production department doing ad layout and paste-up. I returned to Trend Interiors, and happened to walk in just as my former boss, Roald Magnusson, coincidentally was reading the letter that legally reinstated me.

His expression was one of bewilderment mixed with mild shock. He forced a thin smile. "Ah, Garrett... yes... we were, uhm, expecting you."

I reclaimed my desk where a young man in a bright yellow sweater had been sitting, who appeared not at all happy to relinquish his spot after two years. It was an awkward moment as I stood nearby, waiting for him to clear out his personal items. He didn't introduce himself. While I was in the army, Magnusson had joined up with an older partner, Don Danziger, who took to me immediately. One afternoon by the backroom carpet samples, he came up to me and asked point blank, "Do you think Roald is a little light in the loafers?" (A common euphemism in those days for 'gay.')

"Well, last I heard he's never been married, still lives with his mother, has a poodle named Fifi, and most likely is having a relationship with that young guy I replaced."

Danziger broke out into a big smile. "It's what I suspected, just wanted to corroborate. Let me treat you to lunch." The interior design business skews heavily on the gay side, and I don't think that Danziger ever felt quite at ease in their presence. He was pretty much old school and once told me, "I like regular people like you."

The perspective renderings of bedrooms, living rooms, dining rooms, and dens I'd been doing were all in watercolor on illustration board. I'd fallen in love with my colored marking pens inherited at the Exhibit Unit, which were quicker, dried immediately and I suggested to Magnusson that I switch mediums. He asked me to work up some samples, but his reaction was negative.

"Too modern," he said, in spite of the fact that his shop was called Trend Interiors. He would shudder at the sight of anything by Charles Eames, or a sleek kidney-shaped teak coffee table, and don't even mention any Bauhaus inspired design. He preferred the stately Baroque, the fussiness of Rococo, and the well-ordered heaviness of Napoleonic campaign-style furniture.

With both of us working full-time, we moved into a two-bedroom duplex closer to the beach, off 19th St. in Costa Mesa. The extra bedroom became my art studio and I experimented in various styles, not yet set on any specific direction. The beach was our weekend getaway and we roasted ourselves like meat on a spit - which I'm now paying the price for. My primary care doctor says that I'm a "dermatologist's project," having undergone six, skin cancer-related procedures so far, including a MOHS. If you don't know what that is, all the better.

Always budget minded, Stella bought a sewing machine to start sewing her own clothes. She was an instant wiz, knocking out a series of sleeveless short-skirted, A-frame dresses using eye boggling color patterns. It was the era of Pop Art, and the brighter and louder the better. She ditched her pantyhose, threw out the hairspray, letting her hair down figuratively and literally. (I can just imagine what her dear mother might say: *What, you go to work without hose?*)

We inherited a skinny cat that showed up on our doorstep one morning, naming it Giacometti due to its wiry, bony structure. I'd never had a pet, but Stella had bunnies and cats as a kid, however I fell for the woebegone cat immediately. The only problem was that Mr. Brian, our landlord, had a "no pet" rule. He came punctually every Friday morning to do lawn maintenance and general outdoor clean-up of his two, side by side duplexes. Before he arrived, we'd stash the cat in our bathroom.

One morning, we forgot to put Giacometti into the bathroom, and it was roaming around our backyard. Stella and I were prepared to leave for work when Mr. Brian caught sight of our cat just as he nailed a gopher and killed it. Brian hated gophers, and had been trying to rid the backyard of them with the old "hose in the hole" flush method, plus setting traps to no avail. By my last count, Giacometti had killed at least three of the pesky critters.

"Wow, did you see that cat!?" Brian exclaimed. "Faster than hell. Just pounced on that damn gopher. Bam, killed it! Do you know whose cat that is?"

Caught breaking the rental rules, I was ready to lie my ass off, but Stella's Minneapolis upright-Lutheran honesty kicked in.

"It's ours," she said calmly.

"He's a great hunter, I'm sure within the month he'll kill every gopher," I quickly added.

Brian frowned, removed his bucket hat to wipe at a sweaty brow and considered my statement. "Okay, okay...I'll let you keep it, but don't let that cat shred my living room curtains or piss on my floors."

26. COCK AND BALLS

After two months, I quit Trend Interiors, much to Danziger's chagrin that there would be one less "regular" employee. I'd decided to go freelance and thanked Magnusson for the opportunity he'd given me when I was originally first hired, to then rehire me (even if he was technically required by law). He wished me luck, most likely relieved I was leaving to reinstate the young guy with the yellow sweater.

The second bedroom now functioned as both a fine art and commercial art studio. I put a portfolio together, mostly of my interior renderings I'd managed to hold on to, plus pen and ink drawings of cityscapes I'd done in Alexandria. As a last-minute attempt to bulk up my presentation, I threw in a bunch of Army cartoons.

I cold called furniture stores and interior design studios, figuring they were the most likely to want freelance work. At the end of the day with no commissions, I stopped off at the Pennysaver to visit Stella to give her a ride home. She was wise enough not to ask if I'd found any work, which would be short of miraculous on my first outing. She introduced me around, and then marched me into her boss's office. "You'll like him, he's cool," she said.

"Jack, this is my husband, Garrett, he's an artist."

"Hey, man, what are you up to?"

"Looking for freelance work."

Jack had a wind-burned face, was rangy with floppy blond hair, and wore motorcycle boots. I showed him my renderings which he quickly reacted to by feigning to fall asleep, but when it came to my cartoons, he laughed out loud.

"Dude, these are bitchin'! I can use something like that."

I was flabbergasted. "How?"

"People are always advertising their garage sales, trying to unload twenty years of unwanted shit. Do me a cartoon looking into an open garage filled with crap." He reached for a Pennysaver, hitting the cover with his forefinger. "Make it full page in black line, no wash or tones, and leave room at the bottom to drop in our logo. Can you do that?"

"Sure. Have a deadline?"

"ASAP, man."

As I drove Stella home, she said, "Told you Jack was cool."

Not only that, he was an experimenter with his facial hair. One week it would be a sinister Fu Manchu, next a goldminer's handlebar, a pimp's pencil moustache, a poet's goatee, a spiky Van Dyke, or a full-blown lumberjack beard. Jack was always happy, which I think was due to drugs. But I don't judge someone just because he's high.

He rode a motorcycle bareheaded, pre-California helmet laws, and one day, took off after work on his chopper into the sunset and was never seen again. Stella's next boss was a 63-year old man in a black suit and tie, who looked like a dour-faced church deacon. Put him in bib overalls, give him a pitchfork, and he could easily have posed for Grant Wood's *American Gothic*.

He was not cool, or ever high.

We liked Guinness stout at our favorite pub with the provocative name, the Cock and Balls. Yet the name was belied by its charming old-fashioned hand painted sign that showed a rooster standing proudly on two cue balls. They had a billiard table, which, unlike pool, I never learned to play. The Cock and Balls had somewhat of a reputation for its rowdy rugby team appearances, rakish cricket players, and other intemperate Brits between jobs, or "on the dole," as they said. One evening, we watched a travel program on an overhead TV. It was about England's castles and other notable palatial structures.

"Bollocks!" someone yelled at the bar for no apparent reason.

Stella waited a beat to make sure the outburst would not lead to anything more serious (there had been bloody noses during certain football matches), but all remained calm. "Ever been to England?" she asked.

"Nope."

"When you went to Europe with your parents, you didn't go there?"

"For some reason, my dad was totally disinterested in Jolly Old England. He said, 'give me the Alps or give me death.'" He loved snow-capped mountains.

She laughed. "You do know I have a pen pal there, right? In Leicester."

This story was just short of the unbelievable. In 6th grade, Stella had drawn an English girl's name, Victoria Niven, out of a teacher's shoebox and they'd been writing each other ever since. That added up to over thirteen years of non-stop correspondence.

"Let's go," she said.

"To England?"

"Well, Europe first, then across to England."

"Okay...we'll plan for a trip."

We went on a crash budget program, saving every dime and nickel we could hang on to. Easy for Stella who came from a frugal family where Nicholas rolled his own cigarettes to save money, and she currently made her own dresses for work. For me, it was a bit more difficult. I had to spend money in order to make it. I constantly ran out of art materials; markers emptied or dried out, illustration board got used up, ink had to be resupplied, pencils wore down to a stub, and so on. I set aside the fine art, quit painting, to concentrate on my commercial freelance business.

Less than a year later, we had enough cash to go for three to four months. We'd fallen in love with the new model 1968 Volkswagen

Bus, the first year it eliminated the split front window in favor of a singular expanse of wrap-around glass. Also, the two side doors that awkwardly opened outwards were eliminated in favor of a nice smooth slider. We made a down payment on the VW Bus at a dealership that specialized in overseas sales, and Stella promptly measured for curtains, since we planned on living in it. We liked our spacious duplex apartment and didn't want to give it up, but neither did we want to pay three months' rent on it as it sat empty.

The problem was solved one day when I was bodyboarding Newport and recognized a friend getting ready to hit the surf. He mentioned how his "asshole money-grubbing" landlord had considerably raised the rent on his beachside pad, not caring if he remained or left. He was looking for a new summer rental, so I explained I was heading to Europe with my wife, and he could rent our apartment for three months.

"Your place is in Costa Mesa? Man, I don't know, I want to be on the beach."

"We're off 19th Street, you'll get to the beach in ten minutes, and it's downhill. I'll reduce the rent to $95 bucks," I said, which was exactly what we paid. "And it comes with a really cool cat." He took it.

With a heavy heart, Stella sold our VW Bug, the most reliable car ever, crisscrossing the United States four times, plus to Minnesota and back from Virginia, without any major problems. But it gave us a nice added cash infusion. It had truly been a magical little car, and now we would move up (and into) its big brother, a brand-new two-tone maroon and white VW Bus.

27. FAHRT

W e landed at the Frankfurt Airport six hours late due to some technical snafu layover in New York. We were supposed to meet a VW representative, but now it was almost midnight. We fully expected that he'd gone home, for a return trip tomorrow. Collecting our two suitcases, we were prepared to sack out and sleep over in the lounge when a man in a neat herringbone jacket, tie, and pressed slacks came forward and offered his hand.

"Mr. and Mrs. Garrett DeWalt, I presume?" he said with a sly grin.

"Yes."

"I'm Ulrich Kaulbach, please follow me."

He led us out of the airport to a highly polished black Mercedes (what, not a VW?) and without another word, drove off. In the car, he turned on a classical music station. Away from the airport, the streets got darker and darker, and we had no idea where the hell we were. Eventually, we arrived at a building with a lit up blue VW logo sign, where our glorious VW Bus shimmered underneath it.

After we signed the appropriate paperwork in his office, he handed me the keys. "Have a good *fahrt*," he said. Naturally I thought he'd said fart, but I was too tired to question him. However, later I learned it meant 'journey.'

"I have a favor to ask. Can we remove the middle passenger seat and store it here?"

"For what reason?"

"We plan to live in the VW Bus, and build a bed in the back."

"I see." He removed his suit jacket, rolled up his sleeves, got a wrench, and did it himself with very little effort. "Anything else?"

"No, thank you, Herr Kaulbach."

We were ready to depart on our magical tour.

Without a map and driving in the days before GPS, we somehow made it back to the main portion of Frankfurt. We parked in a residential side street, where Stella got busy installing the curtains she'd made, which fit perfectly. Dead tired, we unrolled our sleeping bags to sack out on the floor for our first night in Europe.

In the morning, we found a combination hardware/lumberyard and I gave a workman at a table saw the dimensions of how I wanted a sheet of plywood cut to size. He scratched his head. "Plywood?"

I pointed to a stacked lot.

"Ah, *Sperrholz*. But I don't know inches."

Of course, we were now in the land of centimeters. He was nice enough to follow us out to our parked VW Bus, and measured the dimensions in centimeters. Cut to size, he walked over to a bin of ready-made, but unfinished, coffee table legs. The Sperrholz slab would balance on the rear seat cushion, but needed support up front, and he screwed in the two legs. He recommended a camping store to buy a mattress or whatever else we needed for the road. I tried to tip him, but he refused. "*Es ist nichts*," he said, wiping sawdust off his hands.

Other than a mattress, a blanket, Melmac plates, some flatware, our most important purchase was a yellow bucket — an appropriate color for midnight relief when we lodged overnight in the side street of a suburban neighborhood, instead of a campground with facilities.

HEIDELBERG

We didn't spend a lot of time in Frankfurt, since we were anxious to get moving. Heidelberg is situated on a hill overlooking the Neckar River, providing a stunning combination of Gothic and

Renaissance architecture. It's also home to the famous Heidelberg University, and we heard that students are a quarter of the population. At one time, pre-World War I, students at the university were known for their sword duels, leaving a facial scar as a result, which was considered a badge of honor. These were the same elite class of students that would join the German officer corps, and go out to beat their enemy: the French. During World War II, dueling was prohibited by the Third Reich that presumably put a stop to it. At least we didn't see any scar-faced students rambling around the cafes in Altstadt (Old Town).

We ate schnitzel chased down with tannenzapfle, a beer heavy on pine notes, and we drank lots of it. I asked a couple of students at the next table over, "Speak English?"

"Who doesn't?"

"Do you guys still have sword duels?"

The table of four cracked up. "Frisbee duels, maybe." He leaned in. "Many of those infamous scars were done at a barbershop."

Stella blinked. "What?"

"Yes, instead of risking getting your eye poked out, they'd pay a barber to do it with a straight razor—right across the cheek."

"So much for the badge of honor," Stella said.

They cheered and bought us a round of beer. "Have you been to the *Schloss*?"

"Schloss?" I asked.

"It means castle."

Another word to add to our new German vocabulary.

Stella made a pun. "In English, slosh means 'getting drunk,' like we are all getting sloshed right now."

They raised their beer glasses. "Here's to getting schlossed, or sloshed, whatever!"

Actually, we didn't have much interest in visiting a castle and stuck to Altstadt, which was a pleasant journey through narrow cobblestone streets filled with cafes and boutiques. Budget minded, we did a lot of browsing and window shopping before we left for Köln (Cologne).

KÖLN

Great cities seem to sit astride rivers. Frankfurt next to the Main, Heidelberg - the Neckar, and now Köln at the Rhine. It has a magnificent, twin-spired cathedral which was, according to what Stella read from her guidebook, "construction started in 1248." As much as we appreciated the old-style Gothic, Renaissance, and Baroque buildings, we craved something more modern for a change.

"Find a place in that book that has contemporary art for us to look at," I urged.

She thumbed through the pages. "Here we go, the Wallraf Richartz Museum."

"Doesn't sound modern, but let's give it a shot."

The museum was close to the river, where I found myself looking at one of my favorite artists, Roy Lichtenstein. As one who'd drawn many cartoons, I loved that Roy Lichtenstein had turned the cartoon form into art. Crisp bold black outlines, oversized Ben-Day dots, bright colors, plus hand lettering made the work very appealing. The painting we were looking at was *Takka-Takka*, a close-up of a machine gun blasting away as a grenade was tossed at it. Even though the caption above it identified the battle as taking place in a tropical location with several leafy green shapes depicted at bottom, I wondered how Germans took to this iconic work of Pop Art. After all, their city had been devastated by Allied bombing during World War II.

Stella read my mind. "The Germans, they're our best allies now, aren't they?"

"Maybe they have no choice, since we have almost half a million troops stationed here."

We also saw Monet, Cezanne, and Van Gogh's classic painting *Drawbridge*.

After we'd satisfied ourselves with 19th and 20th Century art, Stella suggested a beer break. Like in Heidelberg, we gravitated to Old Town which was filled with shops and cafes. At the bartender's recommendation, we drank Kolsch beer. He explained, "This brew is somewhat of a merging between an ale and a lager. You like it?"

"Ja," we both said. Kolsch was served in tall skinny glasses and, as we were to find out, it seemed that every beer was served in its own particular shaped glass.

"You know, we should buy some 4711," Stella said.

"The perfume?"

"No, it's cologne, famously made right here in the city, called Kolnisch Wasser by Germans, or eau de Cologne by the French. It comes in a beautiful bottle. As we travel, you often don't get a chance to shower, and you might want to use some 4711."

"Are you saying I smell?"

Stella hoisted her glass, "Another Kolsch, please."

AMSTERDAM

There are many touristy things to do in canal-centric Amsterdam. High on the list, of course, is a canal boat cruise which gives you a unique, low view upwards of the surrounding quaint buildings. The boat tour guide spoke with a microphone, and pointed out that the extended short I-beams with a hook dangling from the top floors were for hauling up furniture.

"In most of these houses, the stairs are too narrow for a couch or refrigerator. I've even seen a piano go up that way to be let in through a big window."

His English was near accent-free, and we decided that the Dutch were the best English speakers in Europe.

"It is said that Amsterdam got its name from combining the river Amstel with dam. Possibly whoever came up with it had one too many beers and confused his 'l' with an 'r.' (Mild laughter.) And speaking of drinking, you are probably asking yourself what if you happen to drive your car into a canal? Well, the city offers classes for that emergency. We have a special city operated pool with a car that is mechanically submerged as you sit inside. At the bottom, you open the window just slightly and let the water pour in. Don't panic! When it reaches chin level, you push the door open and swim to the top. If you try to open the door the minute you submerge, the water pressure will surge in and most likely drown you. Can I get names for volunteers to practice this?"

We watched people literally sit on their hands. I can imagine doing this in the clear water of a pool, but at the bottom of a murky dark canal, and possibly drunk — who wouldn't panic?

The next big tourist item is eating *rijstafel*. According to Stella's book, this style of cuisine was inspired by the Dutch having colonized Indonesia at one time — no longer, since 1950 — and literally means "rice table." What our restaurant served up was a tableful of eleven small dishes of spicy meats, vegetables, and condiments all centering around, well you guessed it — rice. Naturally, we drank Amstel beer.

It was late and our next morning's stop was the Heineken Brewery. We parked across the street from the multi-story squat brick building under a leafy expanse of trees right by a canal, mindful to tightly set the parking brake. *Would a VW Bus float?* I asked myself as we quickly fell asleep. The brewery opened at nine in the morning for visitors.

Stella had a little windup alarm clock that she'd set for eight-thirty, so we could have time to make ourselves presentable. Next morning as she applied make-up and did her hair, I discreetly emptied our yellow bucket contents into the canal. I'm pretty sure brewery tours were slated for that early hour to keep people from overindulging. But we tried our best.

The first thing that hit us was the beery smell. Imagine going to work here until retirement, inhaling those fumes daily. Maybe kind of cool at first, but what would it be like ten years later?

The beer making process was way more complicated than we'd imagined, although the actual ingredients were few. "We only use three things," our guide said, "malted barley, hops, and water."

"I hope it doesn't come out of the bloody canal," a Brit behind us whispered.

"Into those three ingredients, we add our secret yeast formula discovered by Dr. Elion, a student of Louis Pasteur."

As interesting as the tour was, we were just plain thirsty to sample the free beer. In the taproom, our Heinekens were accompanied by cubes of gouda cheese with a side of spicy mustard. Eventually, we were politely asked to leave when we were the last ones left. Back we went to our home on wheels for an extended nap. After a relaxing nooner, we drove to the Rijksmuseum.

We saw more Van Goghs than we'd probably ever catch in a lifetime, including one of his seminal early works, the *Potato Eaters*. It's a grim piece depicting a peasant family in murky dark tones, assembled around a table eating, well…potatoes. Most likely, they had potatoes for breakfast and lunch as well.

But what we really considered the top prize in the collection was Rembrandt's *Night Watch*. This stunning group portrait of a militia, painted in Rembrandt's detailed Baroque style, is twelve by fourteen feet. We looked at it for a long time, eyeing the interplay of light and shadow called chiaroscuro, and wondered about the little girl highlighted in a bright golden dress with a dead chicken strapped to her middle. About seven years after our visit, an unemployed school teacher slashed the painting a dozen times with a knife he'd brought with him from a restaurant, claiming, "God told me to do it." It took four years to repair. In Biblical terms, that was longer than God created the Earth.

ANTWERP

Roughly a two-hour jaunt from Amsterdam, we arrived in Antwerp, Belgium. Here, the river running through the city was Het Scheldt which emptied out into the English Channel. The city center's two big plazas are anchored by an ancient, single-tower cathedral called (in Flemish) *Onze-Lieve Vrouwe Kathedraal*, or Cathedral of Our Lady, meaning St. Mary. It was started in mid-thirteen hundred and all work stopped in 1500. The Gothic structure is not considered to be "completed," since the second tower and spire was never added.

To go from the sacred to the profane, prostitution in Antwerp, like Amsterdam, is legal, but within constraints. Streetwalking is strictly forbidden. The working women all gather on a side lane near the busy railroad station, where they occupy small downstairs flats with street side windows they can pose behind, in various enticing stages of undress. This is the Red-Light District. Commercially, it makes sense. Depart the train, knock back a few tasty brews, bang a hooker, and be on your way. And if you feel guilty afterwards, you can always drop in on the Cathedral of Our Lady and pray. And if you have the urge to urinate, there are (although, hard to believe) two exposed outdoor public urinals attached at the back of the Cathedral. Yes, I couldn't resist peeing against one of the two white marble slabs, stinky as it was.

Both of the main plazas, the Groenplaats, and the Grote Markt, are ringed with pleasant pubs teeming with very happy patrons. Drinking beer in the Northern Flemish part of Belgium is more or less considered national sport, right up there with voetbal (soccer). We asked the bartender what local brew he recommended, since there were many unfamiliar beers listed on his chalkboard.

"De Koninck."

He poured us each a *bolleke*, which is the term for the round, bottom style glass De Koninck is served in. It's a dark amber ale with a surprisingly full, beige head.

"Delicious," Stella said.

"Absolutely," I nodded, thinking I'd love to have a refrigerator stocked with it.

"Where did you two come from?"

"Amsterdam."

"And I suppose you drank Amstel and Heineken?"

"Yes."

"It's piss. Pure piss! The Dutch make horrible beer. In fact, those *kaaskoppen* (cheese heads) take the train to Antwerp just to enjoy the cafes and drink our beer!"

Compared to my De Koninck, I'd have to agree.

"Look, De Koninck is only 5% alcohol, so let me move you up the ladder to sample some stronger beers."

The rest of the evening became a blur as we barhopped the two plazas and attempted to mimic Flemish. "Kust mijn kloten" sticks in my mind, which we repeated several times as we staggered from pub to pub. Finally, somewhere before the sun came up, we crashed into our VW Bus. In between all that carousing, we did manage, however, to scarf down mussels with frites, a local staple, to absorb all that delicious high alcohol beer. It was also suggested we eat *paling* (eel), but we passed.

You can't leave Antwerp before visiting the Rubenshuis, the very manor/studio with a beautiful indoor courtyard where the Baroque master, Peter Paul Rubens lived. It was also a workshop of immense proportions. Rubens was a highly popular and sought-after painter, with multiple commissions to fulfill from royal courts across Europe. He hired students and other master painters to do the journeyman's work — backgrounds, foliage, assorted animals — while he concentrated on the final figures and portraiture. Rubens was a polyglot, and it was said he could engage in a conversation in one language, dictate a letter to his secretary in another tongue, and paint at the same time. He also had a very stunning second wife, the very blonde, nubile Helena Fourment, whom he married when she was sixteen as he was in his fifties. He painted her au naturel, partially wrapped in a splendid stole, which in Flemish he titled "Het Pelsken" (The Fur Coat). She looks splendidly "Rubenesque."

We left Antwerp, drove along the coast going through Oostende - the longtime home of expressionist painter James Ensor. In his early years, the quirky painter's art was labeled everything from scandalous, anarchistic to dangerous. His huge painting *Christ's Entry Into Brussels* was mocked for showing Christ riding astride a donkey, surrounded by leering masked revelers and shady politicians. Even though Ensor was an atheist, he identified with Christ as a victim. The painting is now in the Getty Center.

The must-eat local dish in Oostende (*tomate ceviche*) is a hollowed-out tomato filled with mayonnaise sauce and tiny shrimp harvested right at the beach by fishermen on huge Belgian draft horses that drag nets across the surf, snagging the shrimp.

Driving into France, we arrived in Dunkirk. Originally, it was a Flemish town named *Duinkerke* - or Dune Church - but through many battles over the years, it became part of French territory and was the scene of the hugely famous evacuation the Brits engineered in WWII. We found a handy spot near the beach, parking for the night at a place thousands of soldiers had once waited to be rescued.

PARIS

Before taking in the immensity that is Paris, we chose a campground on the outskirts near a river. Unfortunately, the desk clerk told us it was only for members of a French auto club. I was beat from driving and happened to mention we were Californians on vacation. That made his eyes light up. To many Europeans, there's something magical about California. We learned not to say we were Americans, but Californians. The whole Ugly American concept was raising its head once more with the amped up involvement of our military presence in Vietnam. Massive student protests were surging in Paris, demanding that the U.S. should pull out.

"Number 48 has canceled, I'll give you their spot, but only for one night. No charge," the clerk whispered.

I tipped him two dollars. A glass of house red wine was about forty cents, so if desired, he could go after work and enjoy five glasses on us. We located spot 48 ready to enjoy the unfolding scene. Along both sides of the sparkling river, cafe lights were strung up, live music played as people slow danced in tight embraces. I felt like we were injected into Renoir's Impressionist painting, *Bal du Moulin de la Galette*. Truly romantic.

One of the annoying things in traveling over country borders was money. We'd crossed Germany, Holland, Belgium, to enter into France. Each country had its own currency where an exchange had to be made. No Euro existed at the time, nor was it in anyone's mind yet to create a common European currency. Banks refused coins and only accepted bills. That gave you a choice to spend whatever coins were rattling around in your pockets on knick-knacks, postcards, stamps, or give it away to the gypsy women who opportunistically stationed themselves curbside, breastfeeding an infant. We saw a lot of breastfeeding gypsy mothers.

Banks or exchange centers took a commission for their service, so each time you got back slightly less than you started with, not to mention the loss of your coins.

We left the campground the next day to head straight for the heart of Paris. Stella located a reasonably priced hotel for us on the Left Bank's Rue Napoleon, not too far from Place St. Germain des Pres, a boulevard famous for its cafes and brasseries including Les Deux Magots, patronized by existentialists, writers, and artists.

"Wow, listen to this," Stella said, reading from her guide, "some of Les Deux Magots' patrons include Hemingway, James Joyce, Camus, Jean-Paul Sarte, Simone Beauvoir, and Picasso."

"We'll definitely go there. I know that *deux* means two, but does *magots* mean what I think it does?"

"Eeew, I hope not."

Our room was on the third floor; and with our two suitcases, we squeezed into a rickety cage elevator that seemingly threatened to snap a major cable any second to send us plunging to the bottom. The room was an airy, spacious corner spread with windows on two sides. The bed had a massive carved headboard which reached nearly to the ceiling, looking like something Hemingway might have cavorted in with one of his paramours. The bathroom had a big, raised-platform clawfoot bathtub with an attached brass coiled shower hose. It was the only time in our married life, we were able to comfortably get into a bath together. For a minute, I thought there were two toilets, but one was a bidet.

"Oh, goodie, now I can give myself a proper douche and flush out your swimmers." She'd recently overheard that: "Traveling hippie girls use a Coke bottle, shake it up, and spray the inside of their pussy as a way of a roadside après-sex douche."

"Well, whatever guy goes down on her next is due for a sweet treat. Um, do we have any Coke handy?"

"You wish."

Our concierge was a chunky, world-weary woman who looked like she was straight out of a 40's French film noir. She did two things nonstop: smoke and talk. The minute she heard us exit the elevator or enter the dimly lit lobby, she started talking to us. All French, not a single inserted English word, her soliloquy could go on at length for five minutes. She'd gesticulate dramatically with her cigarette hand scattering ashes over her worn marble countertop as we listened politely, but dumbfounded.

St. Germain des Pres did not disappoint as we strolled the boulevard. For entertainment, there were fire breathers, jugglers, acrobats, contortionists, guitarists, and even a young girl doing a fairly good Édith Piaff impression. A hat or cigar box was passed around for donations by the entertainer or a cohort after an act.

At Les Deux Magots, I told the waiter I had two questions, "We like beer. Is there a good French brew?"

"Oui, monsieur, I recommend Kronenbourg 1664 - that's the year it was first brewed. Second question?"

"What does Magots mean?"

He smiled and pointed through the window to the inside where we could make out two dark squatting figurines sitting atop pedestals. "It means squatting Chinese, um, how you say... alchemists? Maybe, 'magicians' is a better word."

"That clears that up. We'll split a Salad-Germain, an order of frites, and two Kronenbourgs."

"Very well."

You can't expect immediate service in Paris, and it seemed to take twice as long for anything to arrive than it would Stateside. When I kept looking around for our waiter, Stella patted my hand.

"Relax, we're on vacation."

Next day, it was the Eiffel Tower, Gustave Eiffel's ode to the strength of wrought iron. (He also designed the armature that holds up the Statue of Liberty.) At 300 meters (or 1,000 feet), the Eiffel Tower is the tallest structure in France. We bought tickets to take the elevator to the first level, and even from there, you get a really great panoramic view of the city. A ticket ride to the very top was more than we wanted to pay and we'd already spent plenty of money the night before at Les Deux Magots.

"That girl her dad was throwing around as an acrobatic balancing act made me hold my breath. If he would've dropped her, her head would've split open on the cobblestones.," Stella said.

"What a thought." Finished with the Eiffel tower, we sought out a side street bistro for croissants and café au lait. "Did you notice all that brown paper glued to the side of buildings?" I asked.

"Yes, what is that all about?"

Our waitress overheard. "I'm a student at the Sorbonne, and during the protests — which you missed by one week — we graffitied buildings with slogans. The cops then come and pasted over it with paper."

"What were you protesting?" I asked, pretty sure of the answer.

"Militarism, using napalm, Agent Orange, carpet bombing in Vietnam, unfair economic policies, the need for more student rights, I could go on...um...are you Americans?"

"Canadians," Stella said, by passing Californians for once, possibly the only fib of her life. After all, who wants to own up to napalm, Agent Orange, and carpet bombing.

We finished our lunch, paid the bill, and walked to a bus stop that took us to our next destination. "Ready for the Louvre?"

"I can't wait to see the *Mona Lisa*," Stella said.

"She's smaller than you think."

But the *Nike* or *Winged Victory of Samothrace* sculpture was impressive at nine feet tall, posed grandly at the top of a staircase.

"Wow, the way the folds of her dress are carved makes Nike look she's in motion, ready to fly into space," Stella said.

In an upstairs hallway, we came across a long row of Rubens' work.

"Please," Stella said, covering her eyes, "nooooo more Rubens!"

By this time, I think we were both suffering from the Stendhal Syndrome — lightheadedness caused by overexposure to great beauty.

We left the Louvre and drove due south for Nice. Some of the landscape reminded us of Southern California, a bit dry around the edges. Two notable stops were ARLES and AVIGNON. Arles was Vincent van Gogh's home for a year where he drank, painted, and argued with Paul Gauguin, then cut off part of his ear as a gift to a hooker. No surprise, she didn't care for the gift, immediately getting banned from the bordello. Avignon at one time, unbeknown to us, was the residence of a succession of seven popes during some sectarian rift with Rome.

Our waiter strongly suggested we swing twenty minutes out of our way to view the Pont du Gard, an ancient two-deck Roman aqueduct. It was an amazing sight. Roman engineering was something to behold.

NICE

It's difficult to avoid the cliché, but Nice is nice. Jane Fonda had a big hit on hand with Roger Vadim's spacey *Barbarella*. Posters of her were plastered everywhere. I tried to remove one from a wall as a keepsake, but unfortunately it ripped, so I left it behind. The beach is a big draw, but getting comfortable on your towel is not the easiest thing to do, making it literally a pain in the ass. It's all rocks without sand. While we were situating our behinds on the rocks, both Picasso and Matisse were still active. Matisse had left Paris to take residence in a grand hotel nearby. Presumably, Picasso might even have dropped in for a chat with his contemporary, a friendly rival.

By today's standards, I suppose you could say they were "frenemies."

BARCELONA

No one sleeps in Barcelona. At least, that's the impression we got. We'd taken a room right off Las Ramblas, a wide pedestrian tree-lined boulevard that runs down to the Christopher Columbus monument at the port. Birds are a big item, and street sellers offer a variety of caged birds for sale. It is said, some people buy one just to let it go.

Like in Paris, there were sidewalk performers everywhere, the specialty of Las Ramblas being human statues. Painted silver or gold, they would hold a pose as if they were Galileo or some famous person. I hated to think they had to wash it all off each night, then reapply the next day. Or do they sleep that way, turning their sheets into a golden or silver sheen?

The local custom was to go out for dinner at eleven in the evening. Later as we tried to fall asleep in our tiny single beds, it wasn't unusual to hear outside revelry, loud buzzing Vespas, breaking glass, and that was at 3:00 am. At night, the farther you walked down Las Ramblas to the port, the seedier it got, eventually turning into a red-light district. We drove past the Gaudi Cathedral which looks like a giant sand castle, but did not go inside. At many intersections, we spotted the black-clad Guardia Civil, a military police force to let everyone know that Generalissimo Franco was very much in control. Our hotel clerk told us that the Guardia Civil was the least civil police force in Europe. Franco was Picasso's nemesis, ever since the dictator had banned the artist from reentering Spain when he'd painted *Guernica*.

VENICE

From Barcelona, we had to backtrack along the Mediterranean through France, with a very short stop in Monaco. There were many Bentleys, Aston Martins, Rolls Royces, parked in front of the casinos, none of which would look favorably upon our plebian VW Bus.

"I wonder what Grace Kelly is doing right now?" I asked.

"Acting like a princess," Stella said.

Alfred Hitchcock had lost a Leading Lady, Prince Rainier had gained a First Lady.

We left Monaco, and continued on through to Venice. No matter how many photos or postcards you've seen of Venice, it's even more unbelievable than you'd imagine. Almost surreal. Over 100 islands are linked together by bridges surrounding canals—small and large, like the Grand Canal. There are no roads in Venice, so we had to leave our VW Bus in a giant parking lot and find a hotel.

We did a lot of walking in Venice, half the time having no idea where we were. As charming as it was, a gondola ride was out of our budget range and that probably didn't include a tip. But we did take the Vaporetto, a much cheaper public water bus, to the Lido where the Venice Film Festival is held. We were told that *lido* was Italian for heaven. Maybe if your film wins the big prize, you might feel like that's where you are.

It's a good thing we didn't attend the first day of the Venice Biennale because protestors swarmed the opening gate, managed to run into some of the galleries, take down paintings, to turn them around facing the wall. As in Paris, they protested against the Vietnam War and about anything else you can think of. Riot police were called in and it took about three days for things to settle down.

In the British Pavilion, we liked Bridget Riley's eye-dazzling Op Art and Francis Bacon's tortured portraits. In the American section, we saw Richard Diebenkorn's painterly, semi-abstracts for the first time (only later to become big fans). We couldn't help but smile at Red Grooms' Pop Art three-dimensional tongue-in cheek installation of downtown Chicago.

"That's exactly what it looks like!" Stella said amused, having been there.

PISA

The Leaning Tower of Pisa is a great lesson in gravity. Located in what is referred to as the Plaza of Miracles, the eight-story bell tower was used as a lookout post first by the Germans, then the Americans during WWII. Stella and I walked to the top which was a very strange experience. On one side, your body has a tendency to pull against the wall, while on the other side, you feel like you're going to get thrust over the side. With no restraining railing, it would never get OSHA approval.

Back down in the Plaza, Stella said she was served the best ice cream in Europe. Gelato anyone?

FLORENCE

We camped on a hill above Florence, which handily came with a laundry room. Other than washing underwear in campsite sinks, we'd done no laundry on the trip so far. An old lady, her face heavily creased, dressed in all black (a widow?) ran the service. We could pick our stuff up the next day. She didn't write down Stella's name or give a receipt.

"Well, if we never get our clothes back, this might be a great excuse to go shopping," Stella mused.

Ponte Vecchio is a covered, stone-arched bridge that spans the Arno River, filled with boutiques, galleries, jewelers, and souvenir shops. Two years before our arrival, the Arno flooded, killing 100 people, ruining hundreds of thousands of works of art and rare books. On one building, there is a white maker posted at 4 meters (13ft.) to denote the height of the devastating flood.

After browsing through what we couldn't afford, we took a look at Michelangelo's *David* - actually an exact replica which stood outside of the real one inside. The fake was free, the genuine copy was not. The only difference between the two was that the genuine *David* did not have a fig leaf covering his private parts. Italian museums are filled with male nudes from the Greco-Roman and Renaissance era. But when it came to showing *David*'s member, that was strictly an inside job, not for outdoor consumption. Larry Rivers, a pre-Pop artist (and Jewish) noted that Michelangelo had made a minor mistake in carving *David*. The master had not circumcised him.

At the Uffizi, Stella fell in love with Botticelli's *Birth of Venus*. "This is my second favorite painting after Renoir's *Luncheon of the Boating Party*."

Titian's version of a Venus was quite a bit different than Botticelli's. Here, she was a lush full-on nude at five and a half feet across, basically life-size, looking the viewer right in the eye, as if she was saying: *What are you looking at?* One hand is delicately placed on her pubic area, and some would speculate the goddess might be pleasuring herself. Ready for a heavenly orgasm?

We got our laundry back, neatly folded, separated by dark and light, and men's from women's. The price was ridiculously low.

CHAMONIX

When Mark Twain famously said: *The coldest winter I ever spent was a summer in San Francisco*, he'd obviously never camped overnight at Chamonix in August. The campsite was near the Mer de Glace, France's largest glacier. During the day, we strolled around in (clean) T-shirts and jeans, but once the sun went behind the mountain, the temperature dropped drastically and we scurried for warm clothes. Out came scarves, turtlenecks, and jackets.

For dinner, we had cold cuts on bread, but we wanted something hot. We found a campsite *friture* that sold French fries by weight, but you had to bring your own container. We lined up behind the French campers who arrived with nice ceramic bowls and even china. It seems that French housewives brought along their whole kitchen to prepare elaborate meals as their men lazed about drinking, smoking, and playing *petanque*. When vacation was over, the women probably needed a vacation to recover. We scooted up in line with our yellow bucket.

Best damn fries we ever ate.

MUNICH

We'd stopped off at Geneva (home of the European United Nations and Red Cross headquarters), that was known for its stunning views of the Alps, particularly Mt. Blanc, but we kept going for an overnight in Lausanne. From there it was through Innsbruck to Munich.

Ask anybody that's traveled Europe about Munich and they'll say: Hofbräuhaus, which is a scene of famous Octoberfest madness. It was late August, mid-week, mid-day, yet the place was pretty crazy as it was. I don't remember word for word what the sign by the entrance stated, but it went something like this:

STEAL ONE OF OUR STEINS AND WE BREAK YOUR ARM!

With that in mind, we took seats at a community table surrounded by boisterous Germans who were singing something what sounded like; "...ein, zwei, zufwa..."

The hardworking waitresses are known for two things: their ample bosoms and their ability to carry twelve mugs of beer without spilling a drop.

In the downtown section of Marienplatz, workers were resetting curbstones with long blocks of granite. We watched for a few minutes and, evidently, it was close to breaktime because a worker in blue overalls went to their work van to return with bottles of beer for the crew. They sat down and drank as pedestrians scurried by, paying them no attention. Business as usual, German style. We were told not to leave the city center without seeing the Glockenspiel at the Rathaus, which had nothing to do with rats, but meant City Hall. We craned our necks upwards at the Rathaus Tower to watch life-size figures of court jesters, musicians, and jousters rotate around to the sound of bells. The whole spiel lasts about twelve minutes and although we didn't catch the whole story, in part it's a celebration of some nobleman who founded the Hofbräuhaus.

ROUEN

We visited Strasbourg (it rained the whole time we were there), went through Nancy, and stopped off at Luxembourg for lunch. According to Stella's guidebook, you cannot leave Luxembourg without sampling *bouneschlupp*, a soupy concoction of green beans, carrots, potatoes, with smoked bacon. We liked it, and got seconds.

Leaving Luxembourg, we headed for Rouen. I've always loved Monet's series of paintings of the Rouen Cathedral facade painted under different light conditions and times of year in his masterful Impressionist style. Since cathedrals don't change, the facades were exactly as he'd painted them, over thirty times during a one-year span in 1892. It was like looking at his painting in life-size.

It was also the location where the unfortunate Joan of Arc was put on trial and burned at the stake at age nineteen.

28. PEN PALS

In all, people on the continent had been very nice. Mention California and it put a smile on their faces. Hollywood, the dream factory—everyone knew it. Sometimes, we were asked if we'd met any movie stars and Stella would say, "My roommate slept with a Monkee." That answer always left them befuddled.

The VW Bus ran beautifully and the only minor problem had been when we entered Strasbourg. As the rain came down, I turned on the windshield wipers and the one on the driver's side flopped loose. I pulled under an underpass, yet before I had a chance to act, Stella was outside with a bobby pin to secure it back into place.

Other than the long-winded concierge at our Parisian hotel that we never understood a word of (I think I heard her mention Andre Malraux once and maybe Camus), I did get my hand soundly slapped in a bakery somewhere in Nancy. I'd pointed to the particular bread I wanted on the shelf behind the counter, but the lady kept reaching for the wrong one. Frustrated, I stepped behind her counter, started to reach for it when, WHAM, I got the slap. But at least it did clear up which loaf I wanted.

Tomorrow, we'd drive to Calais, put the VW Bus on the ferry, and head across the English Channel to visit Stella's pen-pal of long standing, Victoria Niven, in the flesh. She lived in Leicester, but first we'd spend a few days in London.

LONDON

The ferry brought us to Folkestone, which was the first place in Europe where a border agent suspiciously peeked inside our VW Bus to ask pointed questions.

"What's the nature of your visit?"

"Visiting a friend in Leicester," which Stella mispronounced to be summarily corrected. (It's pronounced as Lester.)

"How long will you be in England?"

"Ten days or so."

"Have enough money?"

Did he think we were in Jolly Old England to panhandle?

"We're in a brand-new vehicle which we have to put gas into, and we do eat three times a day and stay in hotels, what do you think?" Stella said.

"Any alcohol?

"There's a half bottle of Chianti in back, you're welcome to a sip."

He waved us through with a scowl.

If we thought Paris was spread out, it seemed that London was even more so. We got a room in a small hotel near Hyde Park, and when the owner saw my profession listed as "Artist" on my passport, he asked if I'd do his portrait for one night's free stay. I agreed with some trepidation. Other than two "serious" portraits of Stella, all my other work had been done as a cartoon with a satirical edge. Generally, the idea is to flatter the sitter, and this guy was old, nearly bald with a craggy face.

He posed in a lobby easy chair, and I did my best in charcoal.

When I handed it over, he took a long minute to appraise it. "Fair enough," he nodded.

Stella was looking forward to a bath (she hadn't had one since our doubling up in Paris), and our room only came with a sink and toilet, or 'loo' as the Brits preferred. The bathtub was down the hall where she had to feed an adjacent wall mounted meter with multiple coins for the hot water. It seemed like a holdover from WWII rationing.

At Hyde Park, we went to Speaker's Corner to listen to individuals opine about one thing or another while standing on a soapbox. We couldn't get into their local politics, so we grabbed two low-slung, park canvas deck chairs for a rest. Within minutes, a guy in a gray shop overcoat told us there would be a charge for the privilege. He wore a coin change device on his belt.

"The Queen owns these chairs as well as all whales, dolphins, geese, and swans," he said as he gave us a paid slip for the hour.

We walked everywhere, also took the iconic black taxis (called "hackney carriage" by Londoners), rode the double decker buses, and we were called "luv" by most people that served us. We visited the Tate, drank Guinness in pubs, and hung out at Piccadilly Circus, which is exactly what it was, although the word referred to "circle." On the steps surrounding the winged statue of Eteros, hippies, vagabonds, day-trippers, mods, and rockers gathered to soak in the vibe and to be seen. We were never sure which were mods or rockers. An article in Time magazine reported that London youth spent the princely sum of eleven dollars a week on clothes. Graffiti, pretty much in its infancy then, was mostly spray stencil work done on walls. What we saw most was: MAKE LOVE NOT WAR, and we did our best to do just that. If you see the VW Bus a rocking, don't come a knocking.

I got a parking ticket on the front window, wrapped in a thick plastic packet to protect against rain. I had not moved our vehicle for four days, and tossed the ticket into the trash without reading it. Stella said I should have kept it as a souvenir.

Stella got her first experience dialing a phone in one of the red booths, but required help from a passerby because of a confusion of coins and instructions to call Victoria in Leicester. "It can be a bit of a tits up if you've never done it before," he said. "Hold my brolly, luv, while I do it."

LEICESTER

Victoria and Kirk were an unassuming couple, somewhat like people in Minneapolis. A bit of a chill had set in and they were both in well-worn sweaters, or "jumpers" as they called them. They lived on the second floor of a three-story apartment in a one-bedroom flat. For breakfast, they served Marmite, a savory paste, on crispy toast. I made a bit of a face at the pungent salty flavor, and Kirk poked me.

"Their own ad campaign says: You either hate it or love it."

"*Love* it or hate it," Victoria corrected. "And it's the Queen's favorite."

They graciously offered their bedroom, but we said sleeping in our VW Bus would be just fine.

I think that Stella expected to give her pen pal a big warm hug when they met but instead, Victoria reached out her hand. "Lovely to meet you...both of you." British reserve.

But British reserve could also be cast aside as we witnessed in a local pub. A guy's unwanted attention was briskly halted when the girl loudly exclaimed, "Fuck off!" He left quickly.

I made a personal faux pas one evening when we were dining (and sobering up) in an upscale restaurant. Asked what I wanted to drink, I replied: "Tea." I quickly saw Kirk and Victoria's faces fall. Victoria later confided in Stella, who then told me, that tea is what they had day in and day out, therefore coffee would have been the preferred treat at a posh restaurant. To politely go along with my choice, they ordered tea.

I found Kirk rather well-tanned for a Brit, mentioning it. He explained he was a glazier who did a lot of outdoor work. After we finished picnicking along a river, Kirk suggested we take a walk to leave the two women behind, so they could talk about whatever they hadn't covered since 6th grade.

"Were you in the military?" Kirk asked.

"Yes, the Army."

"What did you do?"

"I was the company cartoonist."

He gave me a look like: *Only in America.*

"How about you?" I asked.

"I was a paratrooper in the Mideast. Sometimes, we'd roust people out of their houses at three AM, and herd them into the town square to let them stand in their underwear as we searched the houses for contraband and weapons. I guess it showed the buggers who was boss. A lot of shite went down. They were a nasty lot."

I didn't bother to ask who the "nasty lot" was, or exactly where in the Mideast he had been operating.

We returned to our wives, and Kirk drove us in his Vauxhall to a canal with a pub adjacent to a lock for barge traffic. He ordered shandies all around, a preferred summer drink. A lot of reserve was dropped, and we thoroughly enjoyed the casual pub atmosphere.

A lady in a raincoat came over, interjecting, "Sorry to butt in, but I couldn't help overhear your American accent."

"Guilty," I said.

"Well you know what they said in England during World War II about you Americans in uniform?"

"I'm listening."

"You were over here, over paid and over sexed."

"Next pint is on me," I told her.

"I'll hold you to it, luv." She walked back to her bar stool.

Victoria and Stella were off to the side, having missed the exchange. Victoria asked, "What was she all about?"

Kirk replied, "Nothing much, she just brought up that Americans in uniform were over sexed."

Stella cracked up, nearly spilling her shandy. "Boy, I'll say."

"Speaking from experience, Stella?" Victoria deadpanned, giving me the eye.

They were a lovely couple, and Stella still writes to Victoria to this day.

29. THE PILL

Back in the States, reality quickly set in as the magic of our three-and-a-half-month European tour evaporated. We'd spent 24 hours a day together, slept in a confined space, yet never once had even a minor argument. I have to say that my beautiful wife's sweet nature was the force that kept us on an even keel. She refuses to get upset.

As one Brit said over a Bass Pale Ale, "work is the curse of the drinking class." Stella got her job back at the Pennysaver, but I was a bit adrift searching out clients. Our VW Bus would not arrive at the Port of Long Beach for about thirty days, so we bought a Yamaha 120 CC motorcycle to get around. Scheduling who had to go where and when was a strain. We each bought a helmet at the dealer's suggestion. "Cheapest insurance for your noggin you'll ever buy."

On Harbor Boulevard in Costa Mesa, I spotted a slick new one-story modernist building called Atta's Interiors. It was on a raised platform, flat roofed, about five feet above the parking lot level, and surrounded by floor-to-ceiling glass windows. Very Mies van der Rohe, it reminded me of the architect's Farnsworth House in Indiana, commonly called the "Glass House."

Atta, the owner, was Iranian (or Persian, as he preferred) who immediately took to my color marker renderings. He was tall, slender, movie star handsome, and always impeccably dressed in a suit. He would become a good client for quite a while.

When we retrieved our VW bus at the port in Long Beach, Stella immediately reached for the glove compartment. It was empty. She'd found the "perfect rock" in Nice, shaped like a giant ostrich egg, and had wrapped it in newspapers to have as a keepsake.

"Dang!" she said. "You'd think they'd steal our mattress or sleeping bags, but no. They took a rock?"

One of the problems with freelancing is that I was either buried up to my neck in work, staying up late, or twiddling my thumbs waiting for a phone call. Sitting in the Cock and Balls, Stella put her hand on mine to calmly say, "You need to get a full-time job."

"Okay...and why exactly?"

"I'm pregnant."

When we returned from Europe, Stella mentioned, "I've been on the pill since I was eighteen, time to give it a break."

I had no disagreement with the issue — her body, her choice — yet, I didn't think in terms of her actually getting *pregnant*. I now rode the Yamaha, searching for work as Stella drove the VW Bus in comfort to her work. I landed a job in Garden Grove at a small ad agency called Abelew Art Studio. I was one of four backroom production artists. The front room was staffed by the owner and creative head, Kris Abelew, with Leslie the art director, Warren the air brush specialist and co-art director, and fronted by Joyce, a pleasant secretary. Ralph Abelew was Kris's father, serving as account manager who came in twice a week to do the books, where he either worked out of the conference room, or at a desk in the backroom production area, ostensibly to keep an eye on us. He smoked a pipe and stank up the place.

My three art production mates were Guenther, Cynthia, and Vicki who was an obese woman addicted to Nyquil, or at least it seemed so since she nipped from the bottle all day until it was empty. Guenther was born here, but his parents had immigrated from Germany right after WWII. Cynthia called herself a PhT. That is, she worked to "Put Hubby Through college, a future landscape architect." Vicki was possibly a manic depressive (when the term was used instead of bipolar) and unfortunately, her drafting desk was right adjacent to mine. She read Marquis de Sade on the sly and asked if I'd read it.

"Not yet."

"You should."

I think she sometimes masturbated to de Sade at her desk.

30. ON GUARD

Whenever I mentioned that my wife was pregnant, I was always asked which I wanted — boy or girl? My answer: a healthy baby, which turned out to be a girl we named Nika. Stella now became a stay at home mom, to busy herself with baby chores. We put the Yamaha up for sale, selling it for the exact price we bought it. I removed the VW Bus middle seat, bolted it onto two by fours, and turned it into a couch. Even though we had a two-bedroom, we moved our bed into the living room and made that empty space into a combo sewing room /nursery.

No longer in the freelance business, I completely converted my studio into a painting space, took my homemade drafting desk apart, dumped it, and bought an easel. I signed up for evening classes at Orange Grove College majoring in art and graduated with an AA degree, paid for by the DOD. (The Department of Defense offered the GI Bill, which I wasn't aware of until a counselor told me to apply. The monthly checks were a great help.)

At Abelew Art Studio, I eventually graduated up to graphic designer from production artist, which was more title than reality. All of us had to do paste-up, cut amberlith, do the camera-ready work on Leslie's concepts, and mock-up the much-despised Yellow Pages ads on yellow paper in pencil. Pure drudgery.

I learned a lot about typefaces, type spec-ing, Photostat techniques, proofing bluelines, print shop directions, color separations, and every once in a while, Kris even let me talk to a client about a new job — only if Kris wasn't personally interested himself. My first direct client job was to design a menu cover for a place called the Dixie Pig. I created a cartoon pig wearing a chef's hat and holding a large barbecue fork. Client loved it. I never ate there.

The offices were on the second floor but there was a downstairs room with a Ping Pong table that subbed as a luncheon table. Almost every last Friday, a representative from SoCal Litho who landed most of Abelew's printing work would treat us to submarine sandwiches from an Italian place. Gene Paretti was Italian, and I think a cousin or uncle owned the sub shop. Kris brought Heineken and we were each allotted one bottle. Gene, not an employee of the agency, would knock back three or four, leave a happy man, often walking away with a new printing order.

The Beatles hit *Hey Jude* came out and I remember playing it at full volume in the VW Bus cruising home on Harbor Blvd, singing along. I think some of my hearing loss today can be attributed to that song, that and the Moody Blues *Nights in White Satin*.

Ralph was at his desk one afternoon getting hot under the collar while berating a client regarding an overdue bill. I could hear bits of conversation about, "sixty days is our limit, then we take you to court," and something about, "sending the sheriff to your establishment to collect what's ours!" He slammed the phone down and went to the front office for a fresh cup of coffee.

He returned and faced us, and without any intro or explanation said, "You know during the Depression, I was a life insurance salesman in the upper Midwest. Sometimes I'd go to a farmhouse, knock, get no answer, yet I could see people at the dinner table. Thing of it was, they were all dead. Know why?"

"Suicide?" the depressed Vicki offered.

"No, dear. Ptomaine. Everyone loves to eat peaches. When they figured out how to can them so you could have them year around, it was hailed as a small miracle. But... sometimes the process was imperfect and it could kill you."

Near the close of day, I looked up from my desk to see Gene Paretti in an Army officer's uniform. I gave him a halfhearted salute. "Didn't know you were a major, sir."

"National Guard. Kris tells me you were in the army?"

"Yes."

"What rank?"

"Spec-5."

"Join my unit and we'll bump you to a Spec-6."

"And how does that work?"

"Well, we meet one weekend a month at Ft. McArthur in San Pedro, also for two weeks in the summer to bivouac out in the field. Of course, if there's an emergency and the governor calls us, out we go."

"What do you do at the Ft. McArthur meetings?"

"Strategize," he grinned. "That is, play poker and drink beer. And we pay you for it. It's a nice way to make some extra dough."

I thought about wearing a uniform once more, even if on a limited basis, but didn't say anything.

"One specific though, you'd have to shave your goatee and get a haircut."

A long pause on my part, which made it a definite NO. But to be polite, I said, "Let me talk it over with my wife."

"You do that." He smiled, "I'll be in the area all day."

"Yes, sir."

31. NON TRADITIONAL

I never did discuss it with Stella because I knew her answer would be the same as mine:

NO. Besides, I was already getting government money from my GI Bill, and I'd enrolled in California State University. Seventy out of my seventy-two community college credits were transferable, turning me into an automatic junior. It felt pretty damn good walking around the art department at a state university.

Next time I saw Gene, I tactfully bowed out, but thanked him for the invitation.

Ralph was at it once more, vehemently berating, I assumed, the same client who was in arrears. I heard a lot of "goddamnits," "you sonofabitch," and "I'll sue your ass from here to Sunday." Even though I was three desks back from Ralph, I could see his face was beet red. Again, he slammed the phone down and slumped forward on his desk. I thought it was a good move. Ease off, mull things over, go to the next client. But Ralph wasn't moving.

Guenther looked over to Cynthia, then back to me.

"You should check out the old man," I told him.

Guenther slowly rose, walked over, and put a finger on Ralph's neck and left it there for a full minute. "*Er ist tot,*" he said.

"What the hell does that mean?" Cynthia said.

As little German as I knew, I got it. "He's dead."

"Ohmygod!" Cynthia blurted. "Someone better tell Kris."

Vicki who'd been busy with her hand, heard the commotion, stopped, and asked, "Tell Kris what?"

"His dad just died," I said.

For an obese woman, possibly tipsy from all the Nyquil swilling, Vicki moved nimbly and quickly out of her chair, as if she was on an important mission. "I'll notify Kris! Nobody move!"

Guenther, Cynthia, and I sat there stunned, waiting for Kris's arrival.

Kris stepped up to his father's slumped body, didn't touch him, and without any show of emotion said, "Everyone take the afternoon off, but be here first thing tomorrow as usual. Meanwhile, I'll have Joyce call the coroner."

Currently, all of my university classes were at night. There was a magical feeling walking around the halls of the art department, looking into various studio classes where students were either displaying art or making it. My first assignment was to bring in a painting, not using traditional media like acrylic or oil.

Mr. Brian had discarded a can of driveway patch, a black tarry goop he'd troweled around into the edges of some cracks. I retrieved the can from the bin and used the leftover to spread over a three by three-foot canvas. I had a can of pink spray paint I'd used to redo a little dresser for Nika, and took my canvas outside where I leaned it against our backyard tree. At different angles, I sprayed the pink paint across the surface making it look like a sunset over a black sand beach.

Students approached the assignment in a variety of ways. One girl, described by a male student as "a hot blond chick," displayed a pure white canvas covered with neat rows of lipstick kisses.

Lon Lagerfeld, our professor, asked, "Are your lips sore?"

She puckered to make a kissing sound. "A little."

Lagerfeld negated one student who had poured varnish over a sheet of plywood. "Nope, can't accept it."

"Why?"

"Varnish is considered a traditional medium, historically used in application over oil paint to give it gloss and preserve it. Bring me something different for next session."

The following student stapled a large piece of black tar paper to the wall, covered in something brown. When he stepped aside, a friend said, "Ted, jeez, please tell me that's not shit."

"Nah, man, it's mud from my backyard."

Lagerfeld didn't weigh in but merely said, "Next."

I was up after a female student who'd used menstrual blood on raw canvas. All things considered, I rather liked it. Looked a bit like a Morris Louis, except in red.

In a British accent, Lagerfeld said, "Bloody well done. Period."

"Thank you," she replied.

I hung my piece, waiting as Lagerfeld got close. "What is this stuff? Stucco?"

"It's tar."

"Tar's black. How come it has a pinkish hue?"

I had to bite my tongue from saying 'spray *paint*,' since paint was a traditional medium, and I didn't want to get zapped like the other guy to redo the assignment. "I used two vials of my wife's nail polish, and poured it into an atomizer, spraying it."

"Cool...who's next?"

32. FROGS

About a week before Christmas at Abelew Art Studio, I went into the front office to talk to Leslie about typesetting she'd ordered that didn't fit the space I was supposed to paste it into. She was on the phone, and held up her hand for me to wait. I looked at a cork board posted with numerous Christmas cards from our vendors, printers, freelancers, clients past and present. Then, one card caught my eye. It wasn't store-bought commercial but handmade in a very recognizable style. The curlicue lettering with the cute little drawing of a reindeer was strictly Stella's creation.

I folded the cover back and read the inside: *Garrett - Merry Christmas, I love you so MUCH, Stella* (followed by a bunch of hearts).

I turned to Kris. "How long has this card been pinned up?"

"Umm, a week or so?"

I was indignant. "And nobody showed it to me first?"

"You're looking at it now."

"Yeah, but this was sent to me, it's personal."

Warren, the airbrush artist who I never liked to begin with, piped up, "Garrett, you are an employee of this company, hence we put the card on the board."

Who the fuck uses *hence*? I thought. "Yes, but this didn't come from a business entity, it's from my wife." I took my card down, tossing the pushpin onto the floor. "This belongs on my desk so I can look at it." I walked to the back room, and two minutes later, Kris arrived with an empty cardboard box.

"Pack your shit. Leave. You're fired."

When Kris stomped out, Cynthia started to cry. "Really?"

"Yes."

"What happened?" Guenther asked.

I started to pack. "Doesn't matter."

Vicki said, "Can I switch to your desk, you have a window?"

"Who's stopping you?"

Guenther came and shook my hand. "It was nice knowing you."

"Yeah, *auf wiedersehen*."

When I pulled up in our driveway, exiting with the cardboard box, plastic triangles and a T-square poking out with her card taped to it, Stella quickly understood. "Get fired?"

"Yep."

As I explained the reason, she said, "If a situation like that occurs, just take a deep breath, count to ten silently, then walk away."

There I was back to square one: jobless and with a two-year old daughter.

So, to mitigate the problem, I took up running.

I was never into team sports like some of my weekend warrior neighbors who'd bust a gut on a basketball half court, or exhaust themselves into a stupor playing handball or racquetball. This is also why I liked surfing. It was a solo venture. But lately, I'd been inspired to read about a floppy haired guy called Bill Rogers, who did not look very athletic, yet seemed to win every race he was in, including the Boston Marathon.

I liked the fact, just as in surfing, it was something I could do by myself and it wouldn't cost a lot. I bought a pair of running shoes, ran in my surfing trunks, and already had plenty of T-shirts.

At first, my goal of four miles was difficult, but I managed to do it all the while trying to figure out my next job move. I still got my monthly GI Bill payment, and we had some money in reserve. I called on Atta again, but he'd sold his interior design firm to open a French-style bakery cafe in Laguna Beach.

I entered my first 10K race, even though I had not run farther than four miles. But I figured an extra two miles wouldn't kill me. I gathered with about 500 other runners in a park in Huntington Beach, and off we went at the starter blast of an airhorn. It was cool and overcast, optimum conditions for running. When I crossed the finish line, I got in a queue at a booth for my event T-shirt. A black marking pen was struck through each runner's bib number to keep anyone from claiming a second shirt. It was a proud, magical moment for me as I held up my T-shirt for Stella and Nika. They both kissed me.

"My hero," she said. "You did it."

I would run into my mid-seventies and at the end of it, I'd collected 167 commemorative T-shirts, covering 13 full marathons, 60 half-marathons, and numerous 10Ks. They're like snap shot photos of each run; all I have to do is glance at the graphic and I can recall the exact run. In the beginning, T-shirts depicted a solo male runner for a graphic, but over time as attitudes changed, female runners started to appear. In its early years, there was even an infamous incident at the Boston Marathon, where male staffers tried to wrestle a female runner out of the race (conceivably for her own safety), because women were considered too "weak" to complete the 26.2 mile course.

About two weeks after getting canned at Abelew, I was on the Peninsula and ran (literally) into Lari Gelt who was also jogging. I knew him from high school, where he was part of a social circle that included parents that were yacht brokers, real estate developers, exotic car dealers, and attorneys, yet in spite of that, he was still a nice guy. Lari had a gym locker close to mine during senior year, and I got to know him. We stopped jogging to talk, and he mentioned he and his wife had bought a boutique on Balboa Island.

"If I remember, back in high school you were into art. Used to draw surfers and funny stuff."

"I work at an ad agency," I said, not letting him know I got fired, was jobless. At home Stella had been making beans and onion sandwiches on toast as a budget stretcher. "But I do take on side jobs."

"Great. Can you draw funny frogs?"

"I'm your man."

33. VOICE OF GOD

Lari and his wife, Christina, owned Bartley's Boutique on the main drag of Balboa Island. Bartley was his wife's maiden name which she kept for "professional reasons." Mainly for the recognizable association with her father: Bartley's Bentley auto dealership.

According to Lari, "frogs are really in this season." It always amused me how someone would declare a graphic style, color, or image as "in." Anyway, if Lari had declared that praying mantises were in, I would've agreed. We needed the money and here I was knocking out frog cartoons in a half dozen different styles on spec.

Lari lived on Balboa Island in a nice bayfront two-story house where I went to make my presentation. He was dressed in pressed Bermuda's, a striped polo, in sockless Sperry Rand dock shoes – the perfect image of a Newport Beach man at leisure. He quickly picked one style he liked and commissioned me to do a set of seven frogs in different poses in black and green. "Green is really in," he emphasized.

"What will you do with the finished art?" I asked.

"Silk screen it onto throw pillows."

"I bet that's really in," I said.

He gave me a look, but took out his checkbook. "I'll pay you half up front and the rest upon completion."

Ah, the magic of my first post-Abelew Art Studio job check. Driving home, I turned on the radio and cranked up the Fifth Dimension's mega hit *Aquarius*. Let the sunshine in, baby!

A couple of weeks later I called Lari to see how the frog throw pillows were doing. "They're hopping off the shelves," he said.

Damn! I should've asked for royalties instead of charging a flat fee.

My next job involved driving a truck.

I received a phone call from a guy called Bert Cohen. "Remember me?"

"You're the carpet guy. You made custom carpets for Trend Interiors."

"That's me. Anyway, I'm moving my operation from Costa Mesa to Yorba Linda. I need someone to drive a stake truck back and forth as we dismantle the shop. Can you drive one?"

Same answer I gave frog promoter, Lari Gelt, "I'm your man."

The stake truck was a flatbed rental with removable wooden sides and a rear hydraulic lift gate. I watched as Cohen's workers loaded it up. The drive takes about forty minutes to Yorba Linda where a couple day workers would unload as I got lunch. My job description was driver, not loader or unloader. The whole process lasted four days and Bert Cohen paid me well, afterward offering to hire me as some kind of shop worker in the carpet business, but I turned him down. *Yorba Linda every day, are you kidding me?* Yorba Linda would become the future home of the Richard Nixon Presidential Library - a good reason for me never to go there. I also decided that being a professional truck driver was not even a distant career choice.

What I knew best was art and design. Instead of freelancing various art assignments, I got a crazy idea: why not start my own advertising agency? After all, I had two years first-hand experience at Abelew and pretty much absorbed the concept of how the business worked. The only thing lacking was a copywriter.

The answer came to me one night over the radio. (It wasn't the voice of God, but close. Many years later, that very baritone voice would do an audio recording of the Bible - several times for several different clients.) I was trying to tune into a local FM jazz station, but got an "easy listening" program adjacent on the dial and recog-

nized the DJ's voice. His name was John Stone, and we'd surfed to-
gether on occasion, but kind of lost touch when I got drafted. When
John went off to university, he said something about majoring in
Radio and Television Journalism.

It sounded like it worked for him — he was definitely on the radio.

I called his station, and although the secretary was, at first, hes-
itant to give his home phone number, I did persuade her I was,
"John Stone's very best friend."

34. WEED

Marijuana was passed around campus like candy at a kid's birthday party. Students gave it to one another as you'd offer someone a beer, and compared to today's cannabis, I'm sure it was pretty low-grade stuff — much of it homegrown, or a cheap Tijuana import. Stella joked that when she worked at the Golden Bear, she'd get high walking into the kitchen as employees and entertainers puffed away.

In my painting class, I sat next to Steve Hendrix who'd fulfilled his non-traditional painting assignment by pouring different melted, colored candle wax on a Masonite sheet. He whispered, "Debbie digs you, man." Debbie was the lipstick artist.

"Steve, I'm married."

"Me too, and I'm banging Janet."

"Who?"

"The Asian chick."

Lagerfeld stopped talking, glared at us, and we stopped talking.

"...what I want is commitment to a single idea. I gave the non-traditional painting approach as a challenge to get you to consider other options," he continued.

Today, a professor might say "to think outside of the box," which most likely would've sounded silly back then. My theory is once office workers were herded into cubicles, thinking outside of the box became the going cliché.

"I'm going to show a series of slides that will cover the following: abstraction, both geometric and biomorphic, realism, stylized realism, photorealism, and Pop. Next week, you will bring in your best effort that covers one of those genres. Then you will pursue that style until the end of the semester with passion and drive."

In the corridor after class, Debbie latched on to me, offering a baggie of weed.

"Thanks, but no thanks."

"Dude, why not?"

I knew that with this gift there would be strings attached. Debbie's offer was enticing, as was she (*hot chick* was an appropriate description), but I was not about to fool around outside my marriage. Even though I was an atheist, it was important to Stella for us to get married in a Lutheran church and I agreed. Saying "I do" to all those vows had to mean something, or why bother at all.

"Didn't Steve tell you I was married?"

"Why should that bother me? But, Garrett, have you not heard of the *sexual revolution*?" she said in a mocking tone.

"I'll let it pass me by."

"Ah, you're no fun."

Most of the students in class were on the low end of twenty, while I was at the high end, putting about seven to eight years between us. Maybe to Debbie's thinking, I was "no fun." Also, I did not know a single student who was on the GI Bill.

I started to leave but Debbie followed, "Look, for gosh sakes, take the damn weed anyway."

"You sure?"

"Yeah."

On my drive home, I thought about Lagerfeld's lecture to follow a single vision with a passion to push to its limits. Over time, I'd experimented with many styles, including realism to the point of photorealism. But I chose hard edge abstraction, using masking tape to make crisp edges. I stuck to a dark palette, mixing acrylic paint with modeling paste to create the same stucco surface I'd achieved with the driveway tar goop. Later, Lagerfeld would say my work reminded him of Ad Reinhardt.

I took it as a compliment.

At home, I showed Stella my baggie of weed.

"Where did you get it?"

"From another student, no charge."

"Any Zig-Zags come with it?"

"I'll get some after dinner when you put Nika to bed."

35. G.I. BILL

I invited John Stone out for a beer at the Cock and Balls to explain my idea of us forming an ad agency. He'd be the copywriter, I'd fill the art director's position, we'd put our heads together to brainstorm ideas, and we'd split profits fifty/fifty. We could get a small office I'd located that rented month-to-month for eighty dollars, which we'd split.

When previously I'd laid out my plan to Stella, she commented, "Worst thing that can happen is you lose forty bucks."

John thought about my proposal for a minute. "Only one thing lacking, clients."

"Yeah, we'll just have to hustle. Actually, if we rent the space, there are thirteen offices in the building and I could create a flier and pass them out as a start."

"What'll we call ourselves?"

"DeWalt Stone."

"Let me run it by my wife."

John Stone had a monetary advantage over me. His wife, Wendy, was a full-time administrative secretary at a junior high school, and he could keep working at the radio station from five to nine in the evening as we started the agency. Our first client came as a direct response to my flier. They were two middle-aged women three doors down from us who ran a counseling service called AFP, or Applied Family Planning. They counseled pregnant girls where to receive the proper health care services and how to make the ultimate choice.

John's headline: ARE YOU PREGNANT? YOU HAVE 3 CHOICES subhead: *Call AFP and let us counsel you.*

The unspoken choices were: keep the baby, give it up for adoption, or abort. What was also unspoken but pretty evident, was that this was about an unwanted pregnancy. I designed it as a poster, because the local paper wouldn't accept it as an advertisement.

I took a photo of a neighbor who was seven months pregnant, turned her face away from the camera, and printed it in an eye-catching magenta, reversing out the copy in white. John and I delivered the posters to college campuses, head shops, record stores, boutiques, and book stores. We entered it in an annual Orange County Ad Directors Club competition and won First Prize in the *handbill* category. DeWalt Stone was on its way.

We moved our office upstairs into a two-room space and John quit his DJ job at KNEW FM, but also snagged them as a client. Obviously, the local newspaper did not reject the FM station ads we created. The day before he quit KNEW, I mentioned to John that I needed a stapler and the next morning, he plunked a nice new one on my desk. I assumed he bought it. A week later, Gary Bensen, owner of KNEW FM, came in to sign a contract with us for a series of ads. During the whole meeting, Bensen kept staring at my stapler. I didn't know the man (John had described him as a pillar of society), so when he left, I asked John, "What the hell was with Bensen checking out the stapler?"

John broke out laughing. "Turn it over."

I did, and on the bottom was the KNEW station logo. He'd stolen it, but we kept the account.

I continued running, moving up into half-marathons, and Stella bought a pair of running shoes but decided she preferred brisk walking, which she'd do for many years.

At university, a horrible event took place. A disgruntled student carrying a guitar case went up to the third floor of the library and unpacked a rifle from his case. He managed to shoot seven people, killing three before he was stopped by a janitor that crept up behind him and knocked him out with a crowbar. Fortunately, it wasn't near as tragic as the shooting from the University of Texas Clock Tower by Charles Whitman who'd massacred 15 people, wounding another 30. It was a much talked about subject in the art department, and student opinion was "shit like that could be expected in a redneck, gun-toting state like Texas, but here in California? Wow, man, that's like, totally surreal. A real downer."

Co-owning my own agency, I was able to set blocks of time aside to take classes during the day, quickly increasing my units.

Stella enrolled Nika in pre-school, where she got a part-time cafeteria job during the same hours Nika was there. With our combined incomes, we crossed fingers that we could financially "hack it," and bought a two-bedroom condo on Newland in Huntington Beach. It was exactly four miles to the beach, a perfect eight-mile roundtrip run.

I started to enter juried art competitions around Southern California, which was a pretty simple process. The two art magazines I subscribed to listed "Call for Entries" sections, and through SASE (self-addressed, stamped envelope) I sent in for the entry form, and in return mail, I included two or three 35mm slides of my paintings to then anxiously await a reply, which would tersely state one of two outcomes: ACCEPTED or REJECTED.

A REJECTED notice would put me in a funk, but the ACCEPTED notices outweighed the former. My *first* first-place win was at an exhibition in Thousand Oaks, a good hour's drive from where we lived. Getting into the exhibition meant a drive up to deliver the piece, return for opening night to collect my $200 dollar prize, and return once more to retrieve the work at the close of the show.

I graduated with my BA and continued on for an MA, still paid by the GI Bill. Possibly, next to Social Security, this is one of the best government programs ever.

36. UKIYO-E

O ur trusty VW Bus took us on many memorable trips. North to Santa Barbara, Monterey, and San Francisco, and south to Tijuana and Ensenada. The peso was ridiculously low in Mexico and I could understand why retired couples were turning into expats to live in various communities along the Baja. They just got a bigger bang for their buck in Old Mexico.

Nika was a perfect little traveling companion. She never asked the irritating "are we there yet?" question. When not admiring the passing scenery, Nika kept herself busy with an Etch-A-Sketch tablet - which she got really good at.

Both Stella and I are blondes, but Nika's hair was on a higher spectrum of blondness altogether. It was a luminescent platinum that bombshell movie stars of yesteryear had, like Mae West, Carol Lombard, and Jean Harlow, except theirs came via a bottle. In Mexico, women would actually stop on the sidewalk, reach out to touch Nika's hair. Nika took it in stride and didn't think there was anything exceptional about her hair color.

People would ask Nika, "How do you get it that way?"

She'd reply, "I was born like this."

My first arrival in San Francisco was a magical experience. Stella had already been there with her roommate Dora, didn't mind a repeat visit, and loved the city no less. It had a kind of splendor that reminded me of a grand European city. The Golden Gate Bridge, the Bay, the hills, unique public transport, plenty of places to eat and drink, distinct architectural neighborhoods, and the San

Francisco Museum of Art (months later to become the San Francisco Museum of *Modern* Art). There was also something else I was
quite curious about - a new museum dedicated to pornography.

With Nika in tow, Stella volunteered to sit that visit out. Even if
it had been only the both of us, I feel her interest level would've
been "no thanks, but you go." And I did.

Well, as they say, a little goes a long way. There was Tom of
Finland, famous for his homoerotic drawings of studly leather-clad
guys which I quickly bypassed.

What I found most interesting was the traditional woodblock
print work of Japanese artists. The erotic prints were referred to as
"Shunga" or "Ukiyo-e," and were often bound together in "pillow
books." These were presented to the bride as "instructional manu-
als" in case they needed to figure out what goes where. The art was
done in delicate line, soft pastel colors, and lots of patterns on
opened robes to give the viewer just the right money shot.

One of my art history classes briefly addressed Japanese print-
making which included the work of Utamaro, mostly about how he
influenced Impressionist artist Mary Cassatt, plus post-Impressionist
artists Lautrec and van Gogh. On screen in class we saw several
slides of pleasant scenics, but not what I was seeing today. Evidently, Utamaro was a master of ukiyo-e, which I guess universities
self-censor from showing.

One of the most astounding Japanese prints (hard to look away)
was of a female diver receiving oral pleasure from an octopus. Figure that one out.

"Had enough?" Stella asked as I rejoined her and Nika in a coffee shop.

"You'll never believe what an octopus was doing to a girl, underwater no less."

"I'll just have to imagine."

Years later, the museum would close due to "soft attendance figures," and "general lack of public interest." When you have a city
famous for strip clubs and live action shows, I guess people prefer
gawking at the real deal instead of two-dimensional images.

In San Francisco, I wasn't looking forward to maneuvering the VW Bus with its manual transmission up, down, and around the city's alarming hills, so we walked and walked some more. Nika never complained, always keeping up with us. For a little girl, she was very energetic. As to be expected, we also rode the cable car. At one point, it got so jam-packed with people that Stella started to fan her flushed face.

"I can't breathe," she said.

I steadied her by the arm and we got off at the next stop, where she quickly recuperated. The three of us ended up in the Tenderloin district on Market Street where we heard a street ska band playing. A crowd of about a dozen people had gathered around a quartet composed of guitar, trombone, saxophone, and a steel drum. Because of Nika's size, she easily started to wedge herself into the front to get a close-up view.

Then, a very muscular pair of brown arms reached forward, picked her up, and drew her inside.

I looked at Stella, and, without speaking, thought: Should we be worried?

"'Scuse me," I said, abruptly shouldering in.

Without missing a beat, all four musicians were staring at Nika. "It's the hair, mon," the steel drummer said.

37. WANG

At DeWalt Stone Advertising, business was doing well enough to move for the third time into a larger space. We hired a secretary and a part-time production artist. On each of our moves, we made sure to have a Newport Beach address. Presenting a business card to a potential new client, we wanted them to know we were in Newport Beach, and that we must be doing something right. After all, advertising is as much about perception as anything else.

One of the favorite parts of my job was designing logos. There's nothing quite like the satisfaction of creating a mark that graphically represents a corporation. Easily recognizable, they embed into our visual culture. Think of the CBS "eye," or the Nike "swoosh," or the Mercedes three-pointed star which the "Peace" sign closely resembles. Later when I taught graphic design in university, I would draw the Mercedes and Peace logos side by side in thick marker pen on the white board, to ask my students which one they preferred to see on the hood of their car.

It was about a 50-50 toss-up. The more aggressive ones that wanted to graduate and make a million dollars before they reached thirty-five voted Mercedes, while the laid-back socially concerned types went for the Peace symbol.

My approach to designing a logo was straightforward. I'd work my butt off to create something I was really proud of, then do two more that would pass muster at a client meeting - presenting them with three choices.

It rarely failed that the client didn't choose the one I had in mind.

At one such meeting with a new client, Vasco Civil Engineering, the owner immediately pointed to the bold, uppercase serif V on my presentation board, where, in the negative space, I'd depicted a plumb bob (or plummet).

"That's a great symbol. Maybe you don't see it at first glance, but then it pops right out," Edward Vasco, the owner, said. "Hey, why don't you go into the back room with Choi here so he can show you something that will be of interest to you as an artist."

"Yeah," Choi grinned, "it's my Wang."

The three other engineers chuckled. "Choi can't keep his hands off his Wang."

I didn't know what I was getting into until I followed the beaming Choi into a back room. "It's a computer that draws," he said. He inserted a rapidograph pen into a little mechanical arm suspended over a large sheet of blank paper. It reminded me somewhat of those things that register earthquake vibrations. He turned on the Wang and I watched as the pen scooted from left to right horizontally, then down a space and reversed course, to keep going.

"It's drawing the topographical depths of a man-made lake we're engineering for a huge new housing development. Saves a lot of drafting." He nudged me, "Better watch out, a Wang might steal your job."

"Does it do logos?"

When it came to creating ads, John and I put our heads together to merge his headline copy with my visual take. Mostly, we were on the same track, and rarely disputed each other's concept. At this time, we had a three-branch savings and loan as a client, and John came up with the idea: "Bigger Isn't Better," to compete with the likes of other large financial institutions. I drew a cartoon of a businessman getting fitted by a tailor for a suit that was obviously two sizes too big. Customers mentioned seeing the ad to tellers, but best of all for us, *new* customers mentioned it.

38. Z

Weekends were for the beach. Nika loved playing in the sand with an assortment of toys, and Stella always brought a paperback. I'd be out in the surf on my bodyboard and look back to see the two of them, flooding me with a surge of warmth. It was so simple and perfect, our little threesome family unit. When I finished surfing, I'd trade off and play with Nika at the water's edge as Stella went in. When she came out of the water, I'd greet her with a towel, admiring her lanky, slick shiny body. I'd read somewhere that if, just before you died, you could pick one day to relive for eternity, what day would you choose?

I thought a day like today would be high on my list, because I knew that later on tonight, after Nika was asleep, we'd make sweet love.

John's domestic life was not exactly humming along judging by bits and pieces of phone conversations I'd overheard in passing. I'd more or less made it a rule that we would not discuss our homelife at work. He had two kids, and I could barely remember their names, not that interested to ask. John and I socialized, but at the office. We had lunch together almost every day (or skip it to do a bit of body surfing when the waves were up), sometimes had a pint or two at the Cock and Balls after work, but that was it. We didn't hang out much after work hours, eight hours a day (or more) was plenty.

His marriage didn't hold and seven months later, he was divorced. Brenda had been his high school sweetheart, now she was his ex-wife. Temporarily, he moved into a small apartment, leaving Brenda his house to whatever the lawyers decided next.

John and I used to joke around about cigarette companies, like what if one wanted to hire us. We were both non-smokers (save for the occasional joint), so on principle, we'd turn the company down. Of course, no tobacco company would ever approach us since they were a multi-million-dollar business, and we were a speck on the wall when it came to being part of the ad world. Much of Orange County advertising was based on real estate promotion and new housing developments that fueled the county's rapid growth. Instead, we stayed away from the real estate business to chase after savings institutions, insurance companies, restaurants (if we liked their food), car dealerships, and small industrial manufacturers.

We hooked up with a dealership that sold Datsuns (later to change to Nissan), where we each got a good deal on a sporty, two-seater 260Z. Not only did we want our clients to know we were Newport Beach based, but we wanted them to see us arrive in a new cool Japanese import car.

Our hair was moderately long, but our goatees were trimmed short. We wore denim or soft leather jackets (mine even had fringe) which meant we walked a fine line between projecting a "creative" image, or looking like two hippies that would flake out and not deliver the goods. In presentations, John was generally the front man. With years of radio announcing behind him, he had a commanding, reassuring voice. I went solo on logo presentations, but in ad meetings John did most of the talking. Rarely was there a question about lay-out, art, or design. The discussion usually revolved around copy. For some reason, every ad Marketing VP thinks he's (rarely a she back then) a writer. No client took it upon himself to challenge any aspect of my design, and John often found himself making copy changes on the fly in front of the client.

"Wouldn't it sound better if we said…"

"Or, let's use the second sentence as a lead-in, I think that would be stronger…"

"Maybe we should include rack and pinion steering at the very end…"

And so forth…

When I parked my brand new 260Z on our dedicated space in front of the condo, Nika was outside on her Stingray, a pink banana-seat bike with the raised handlebars. She took one look at the silver coupe, and screamed, "Daddy got a new car!"

Stella stood in the open doorway in frayed, cut-off shorts and a striped braless tank top, looking quite fetching. She knew the car wasn't a personal purchase. "How much did that set your company back?"

"We got a discount."

"We?"

"John got one too. His is blue."

"Oh boy, to match his eyes I suppose."

Later over dinner, Stella teased me that John and I were like Sonny and Cher with their matching Mustangs.

"But they'd be Sonny and Sonny," Nika piped up.

In 6th grade, Nika decided to run for president, not of her class but of the whole grade school. She said she was doing it out of "payback." Another girl with an almost identical name, *Nica*, had declared for president.

"I can't stand Nica, she's always talking about riding horses at summer camp, taking boating trips to Catalina, and the worst, she takes private calligraphy lessons. I am going to beat her like a bongo drum."

"How can I help?"

Nika wanted to make "cool" posters for her election, requesting thick paper, brushes, and paints, which I supplied for her. I turned over my one-car garage studio and she got busy painting rainbows, unicorns, smiling sun faces, doing a great job hand lettering. She refused to let Stella or me help out. "I want the art to look like a kid did it, not an art director or a clever mom."

Her motto: Vote NIKA with a **K**!

She won.

On the day of her inaugural, parents were invited into the school's front lobby where about seventy folding chairs had been set up. It was a full house. Nika, dressed in a fluffy little white dress with a spotlight beaming down on her hair, literally glowed.

I overheard someone say, "She looks like an angel."

Nika tapped the microphone, introduced herself, thanked the students for voting for her, and delivered a concise, smart speech any president would be proud to deliver.

It was magical.

39. ASSEMBLAGE

Everyone was throwing parties, serving up cheap red wine and weed. We figured, if others were doing it, we wouldn't have to, so we went with the flow. One of our favorites was hosted by Glen and Celine, a doctor and his wife, but theirs was definitely not of the cheap wine variety. They owned a rambling two-story beachfront home on the Balboa Peninsula and organized their parties by mail. Each late spring, we'd receive an invitation that listed four Sundays, spread out over the summer, to become known as Celine's Sunday Suppers. You could go to one or all, depending, but you had to phone first to find out what food item to contribute. It was a potluck set-up, and Celine didn't want to end up with four Cesar salads or multiple trays of brownies. You also had to bring your own meat choice. Glen had a double-decker barbecue, mastering the simultaneous cooking of fish, chicken, bratwurst, pork chops, and burgers — giving each its proper grilling. Strictly culinary magic on Glen's part.

Both Glen and Celine were into art, and were regular art museum attendees which gave me a mutual area of conversation. They'd been inspired by an Ed Kienholz assemblage exhibition and wanted to do something like it, but as a group party effort. Glen drove several sturdy fence posts into the sand in front of the house, and linked them up with sheets of plywood. In our latest invitation, we were instructed to bring "a throwaway item bigger than a breadbox but smaller than a VW Bug that could be attachable to a wood surface."

People brought all sorts of unwanted bric-a-brac that, with the help of a cordless drill or power stapler and massive amounts of carpenter's glue, was attached to Glen's pre-set armature. Baby shoes, busted wicker-chair backs, a Tijuana bullfight poster, a crushed lampshade, a mannequin hand, a torn swim fin, bicycle wheel, several abused Hawaiian shirts, and objects that were just not readily identifiable got stuck in place. You could say the composition was helter-skelter. There were gallon cans of acrylic house paint, mostly tail ends, and it didn't take long for party goers to have as much glue or paint on them as the assemblage warranted, since we were concurrently drinking and creating. At the risk of upsetting the majority of Republicans (after all, it was Newport Beach), I painted a large caricature of Richard Nixon.

Bart Fairmont, a Democrat (one of a few) and geologist, stepped back to admire my portrait. He dipped his brush into a can of red paint and slashed it across Nixon's face. "Take that, DICK!"

This was at a time when (ex-president) Nixon was trying to re-invent himself as an erudite worldly statesman, but certainly blowing it for all surfers when he took a walk on the strand of his beach-front property in a suit, tie and highly polished black shoes.

One hard and fast beach rule: Whatever you bring to the beach, you take with you as you leave or trash it. Technically, to let our as-semblage stand in place for the next Sunday session would be illeg-al, and beach maintenance would tear it apart. When sundown hit, we carefully dismantled it to store it in a catch-all room off Glen's kitchen. Next party time, up it went again to continue the process. I think it was the only summer that nearly everyone came to all four of Celine's Sunday Suppers, just to see what the finished product would look like. At the grand finale, people gathered around to snap photos of our spontaneous assemblage which had taken on the hue of a small happening. Maybe our effort wasn't a Kienholz worthy installation, but it had been a hell of a lot of fun. It was a one-time summer event never to be repeated. Yes, magical.

Since Glen and Celine were in a higher income bracket than most of our other friends, it wasn't gallon jugs of mountain red wine, but instead, mix-yourself cocktails. Neither Stella or I drank hard liquor, but the provided brands all appeared top-shelf to me. Gin was perhaps the most popular. There was a handy blender if you wanted to make gin fizzes. Weed was less common, but a joint was passed around now and then. We brought our own beer and took Nika along, in a day when few people did that. Back then, the idea was to get a babysitter so mommy and daddy could party, use uncensored language, get crazy and hammered (no such thing at that time as a designated driver), without having their impressionable children witness the adult activities. One evening, someone removed a fire extinguisher from the stairwell and, well, extinguished everyone within range. It was taken in stride. There would be occasional dramatic spats, resulting in divorces, which left the ultimate Dear Abby question: which ex would continue to attend the parties?

Maybe by today's standards, people might think that bringing a young child — especially a girl — into all this beachside wildness was bad parenting, but we survived and thrived. Nika did not suffer any post traumatic party syndrome.

Today at these very same Celine Sunday Suppers, our friends bring their adult children as well as grandchildren, as we all sit around, quietly behaving and sipping Merlot or Chardonnay while discussing the universities their offspring attended. They talk about exotic trips to locales like Borneo, or Yucatan. We heard one guest say, "...boy, if you thought there were a lot of steps to the top of that Chichen Itza pyramid, try hiking Mt. Kilimanjaro." For a tease, Stella threw in how her father had once been trapped on an ice-floe surging down the Mississippi River, to get rescued at the last minute from a bridge before plunging over a waterfall to his certain death. *Great anecdote, Stella!* I mentally cheered her.

That brought quiet reflection and a switch of topics to everyone's medical maladies, which changed the atmosphere into an environment that resembles a wellness center retreat. The liquor bar is no longer in business, having been replaced by a row of various wines and one large silver decanter filled with Celine's wine of the day, plus a bucket of ice with bottles of Sierra Nevada for the few who don't drink wine.

That's me, party of one, please.

Oh, really good news — no one smokes anymore. And who misses that?

If one is not in the mood to engage in conversation out on the front patio, the sidewalk provides a very watchable transit for skateboarders, roller bladers, joggers, speed-walkers, Segway riders, bicyclists, gawkers, and one unhinged, severely-tattooed guy who stopped to announce he was a "good friend of Sonny Barger, head of the Hells Angels!" None of us said anything, but Celine stepped forward and offered him a tray of hors d'oeuvres. He chose a toast point with Camembert.

For Glen and Celine to host these ongoing parties summer after summer and turn their home over to twenty (or more) people is really commendable, which takes a good-natured, tireless temperament, and a willingness to accept occasional chaos and upstairs shenanigans. (There are five bedrooms.)

But what I personally found quite satisfying is being able to look at my own abstract painting that Glen and Celine purchased. There is no assigned seating once dinner starts, so I always try to position myself at the dining table across from where my piece is hung on the wall, nicely spotlighted too. Two other families also bought my paintings but they don't throw parties.

40. CELEBRITY STAMP

A funny thing happened on the way to my MA graduation: Lon Lagerfeld offered me a faculty position. Maybe it was more unexpected than funny? My art professors knew I was an art director at my own ad firm, and I was asked to teach a session in 2-D Design.

In September, I would return to campus not as a student, but as an instructor with no instructions given on how to do it. They were pretty lax times, and no department head ever reviewed my lesson plan, or syllabus, although that would follow in the ensuing years. People would later ask what I had done in order to teach art at a university.

My answer: Graduated. *

Almost from day one at DeWalt Stone, I bought a 35mm camera to take slides of the work I was most proud of. Every art classroom in the department had a Kodak carousel stashed in a cabinet, which I found to be the perfect teaching tool. As a brand-new teacher, I had one small detail in my disfavor. I did not have a backlog presentation of previous student work my class could aspire to. I introduced myself as an art director/co-owner of DeWalt Stone, lowered the blinds, turned the lights off, and instead of previous student samples, showed a half-hour slide presentation of my work.

With the lights back on, I saw a lot of startled expressions.

"Is that what you expect us to do?" a student blurted.

"Sure...no, I'm joking. But the basic principles you'll be challenged with can easily be applied to what you saw on the screen."

I handed out a materials supply list, giving them a few minutes to study it. "To help you out, I've brought all of those art items for a show-and-tell so you can see what everything is. Do not, I repeat, DO NOT, hand that list over to an art store employee and expect them to find it for you."

"How much is all this shi-, err...*stuff* gonna cost?"

I smiled, "You were going to say 'shit' weren't you? Anyway, around fifty bucks."

"Wow!"

"Granted, education can be expensive. But you know what will really cost you? NOT getting educated." I motioned with both arms to invite them forward. "Everybody step up to my desk please, so you can see firsthand what these items are."

I transitioned easily between art director at the agency and art instructor at university. During a demo on the 12-step color wheel, I mixed red and yellow paint. A female student practically screamed, "Ohmygod, that makes *orange*!"

"Wait 'till you see what I can do as I mix yellow with blue. Any idea?"

"No. Do it!"

For a final 2-D class project, I had students** bring in a magazine reproduction of a celebrity they admired, to transform into a U.S. postage stamp design. Imagery on stamps back then was pretty stodgy: portraits of Dolly Madison, Helen Keller, or engraving-style art of the Liberty Bell, the Capitol, and one that showed two violins. I wanted to make the format contemporary, moving away from the traditional style. I showed students how to grid off their photo image, then transfer it to illustration board where they would reproduce it in ink pen, and add one color of their choice.

The response was enthusiastic. Students brought in images of Elvis Presley, Marilyn Monroe, Cat Stevens (now known as Yusuf), Tom Petty (I had no idea who the hollow-cheeked kid was), Johnny Cash, David Bowie, Blondie, and many other idols of the day. Even the student who was amazed that yellow and red make orange, did a superb "I Love Lucy" stamp, using a bright orange background.

I installed their work in a lengthy hallway display case. On my next walk past the case, I saw a crowd of about a dozen students and a couple of instructors eyeing the work.

"Wouldn't it be cool if the Post Office actually had Elvis or Monroe stamps?" a student mused aloud.

"Hah, get real" an instructor huffed, "that will never happen."

Now, years later, the Post Office has issued about every celebrity you can think of, including most of the ones my students created...although I'm still waiting for Tom Petty. Recently, Stella brought home a block of Marvin Gaye stamps. He's wearing a colorful beanie and appears to be singing.

Perhaps: *What's going on?*

* *Across campus at another division, a guy named Kevin Costner was picking up his sheepskin same time I was. Never met him, though.*

** *One of those students was a professor I'd had for philosophy who took my class because he was interested in "visual aesthetics". A woman he dated was two-timing him, and when he foud out he bought a gun and shot her other lover. The professor was given a life sentence in prison.*

41. LACMA

About a year later, I ran into Deborah who'd done her first project in lipstick kisses. But the so-called muse Lagerfeld had wanted us to follow, in her case, ended up being swimming pools. Realistically painted, always at night with underwater lighting, and featuring a solo female swimmer, her work projected a dreamy Southern California aura.

I was getting coffee in Laguna's Zinc Cafe (I Zinc, Therefore I Am), and she invited me to sit with her. "What are you up to these days, Garrett?"

"Teaching 2-D Design, part-time."

"That's it?"

"No, I'm also a partner in an advertising agency."

"How about your abstract painting, give that up?"

"Never."

"Where do you show?"

"Currently, I don't."

"Do you sell?"

"Occasionally. I enter juried exhibitions and have won a few monetary awards."

"Doesn't toiling in the trenches of commercial art conflict with your fine art?"

I sipped from my oversized, white ceramic bowl of latte. "Not really, the commercial art supports the fine art."

"I see," she nodded. "I really liked your master's exhibition, much more color, and a looser approach, a bit de Kooning-esque, if you don't mind me saying so."

"I consider it a compliment." I didn't tell her that Lon Lagerfeld had once said my work reminded him of Ad Reinhardt; so, I'd graduated from restrained dark hues to colorful splashy hues.

She leaned in. "Let me give you a tip."

Possibly the best tip I ever got.

Deborah had a full-time job teaching painting at a community college that heavily promoted realism, her specialty. She told me she'd applied and was accepted to be a member of ARS at LACMA, which I'd never heard of. I knew LACMA, but not what ARS stood for.

"It's the Art Rental & Sales Gallery, an independent non-profit organization within LACMA that represents artists of all ages. They have a stable of one hundred artists that each bring in two pieces. One piece goes in the rack, the other is displayed in adjacent gallery hallways. When a piece goes out the door, they call and you bring another."

"You said rental, how does that work?"

"Most corporations, instead of individuals, prefer to rent. The minimum is six months, but many extend to a year or even more. You receive payments graduated to your price level. They take 25% of rentals or direct sales."

"How do I get in?'

"Call Sally Henderson...here, I'll write down her number at the museum. Tell Sally that I recommended you. For the interview, she'll have you bring one piece and a slide packet of twenty samples." She blew me a kiss and left. "Good luck."

I waited a week before calling. What if Sally rejected me? This was like a juried exhibition, but on a museum scale in the hallowed halls of LACMA.

I remember one painting instructor telling the class that, as an artist, the most important thing to learn was: *accepting rejection.* With that in mind, I didn't tell Stella I had an appointment at the LACMA ARS Gallery, and drove off with what I considered my best painting. If I got rejected, I wouldn't have to tell her and suffer defeat twice, although I'm sure she'd give me positive feedback.

The gallery was downstairs in the Bing Center and as I carried my painting through the halls, I slowed to gauge the work of other artists on the walls. It was an eclectic display. I guess they wanted to cover all bases, and I saw Pop Art, minimalism, photorealism, collage, abstraction of every stripe, landscapes, still lifes, and even a few large charcoal figure studies.

I opened the ARS office door. "Hi, I'm Garrett DeWalt, is Sally here?"

Sally was a slim blond who sat cross-legged in a kind of lotus Zen pose on an ergonomic chair in front of a View-Master, obviously checking out artist's slides. On the far wall was a floor to ceiling rack stacked with paintings, only their edges visible, but with an attached piece of masking tape that had last names written in bold black marker. The work was alphabetically stored.

I'd wrapped my painting in opaque plastic sheeting, not so much to protect the surface, but more to add a little drama of revealing it.

Sally swiveled around. "Well, take it off."

"By all means, do," two other attending ladies said with a sly grin.

I ignored the double entendre, removed the wrapping, and held it up at eye level.

"Okay, that's fine. Yeah, great. Love it. Lean it against the rack. Bring one more piece at your earliest convenience. Got slides?"

"Yes."

"Good. Come here and fill out this form."

That was it. I'd been judged and was in! I would have a long-standing and lucrative relationship with the ARS Gallery until the day they closed. Those years were magical. Sally was a real fan of my work, always doing a great job promoting it. Every time I dropped off a painting, or sometimes two, I got a visitor's pass that gave me free access to any part of the museum to wander about in all its myriad galleries. I saw some terrific one-person exhibitions. David Hockney, René Magritte, Georg Baselitz, Lee Krasner,

Wassily Kandinsky, and whatever the permanent collection was on rotational display.

With the addition of my teaching salary plus the ARS Gallery stipends, we eventually made another move, our final real estate purchase. We bought a condo in Irvine, unbelievably only two blocks away from the man-made lake that Choi's Wang had engineered. I would spend many years running around that lake thinking of an excited Choi watching his Wang. Whatever happened to Wang?

Nika was now almost twelve years-old, ready to enter junior high next year. Settled into our new Irvine home, over dinner Stella announced to both of us, "I'm pregnant."

"Wow! Mom, I hope it's a boy. I always wanted a brother," Nika quickly responded.

I was speechless; however, her doctor wasn't. "You're an older woman now (she was 39) and you're going to have to take it easy; after all, you did have a miscarriage a couple of years ago."

In California years, 39 is older. If she was a movie star, she'd be playing a grandmother.

42. TRAINED

Our agency was humming along and we hit several peak income years. We had a great secretary, Antoinette, who was terrific at coercing clients in paying overdue bills, and did not implode like Ralph had at Abelew Art Studio. She was soft spoken, and over the phone, would say things like, "You know I have some shopping to do near your company, why don't I drop in and pick up a check?" It worked every time.

One of our profit centers was the 15% rebate. We charged for creating the ad, then placed it in a newspaper or as a radio spot. When we received the bill, we were rebated 15% by the media, while we billed the client the full amount. Kind of like free money. An ad, on contract, could have anywhere from six to a dozen placements, all the while earning us the rebate just for Antoinette typing an invoice and the cost of a postage stamp.

John had promoted radio advertising to our clients, which worked well because he personally did the voice over, saving us from having to hire talent. He did have to buy recording studio time, but that was factored into the client billing. Sometimes, I'd be driving along on the San Diego Freeway in my sporty Datsun Z to catch one of John's commercials, thinking: *Hey that's money in our pocket.*

My logos somehow attracted attention from a Japanese publisher that produced a thick volume of international logos, selling at $100 bucks a copy. I had seven entries, the most from any single designer.

The slick hardback was prominently displayed on our conference table during client meetings. While browsing, I would see it on the shelves of the big corporate bookstores.

Occasionally when my hair got a bit shaggy and my goatee needed a trim, a potential client might have his doubts about me and would ask: *What are your qualifications?*

My reply: *I have an MA in art, teach design at a university, and my work is published in that book in front of you.*

Enough said.

An art supply store where I bought my materials for the agency had a dedicated stand-alone room to display commercial art, showcasing designers, photographers, illustrators, even architects on occasion. The owner asked me to mount a DeWalt Stone exhibition, getting me immediately busy matting and framing our graphic work. Logos, ads, brochure covers, and posters were interspersed with a half dozen ad awards we'd won.

The work was up for a month and two things happened: I got over a dozen calls from freelancers that wanted an interview to present their portfolios. The other was a new client, who was the least likely person we expected to add to our roster. In fact, his business was something we'd never even considered to pitch.

His name was Dr. Brent Young, and he was a dentist.

He also owned a dental lab, but it wasn't his lab or dental office that he wanted to promote, it was his "practice management seminars." We were in our conference room with Antoinette behind us taking notes as Dr. Young explained the business, which was a good thing since neither John or I were clear what it was about.

"I give motivational talks in hotel conference rooms to dentists on topics like having a more efficient front office staff, how to tactfully suggest dental upgrades to clients, to not shy away from recommending cosmetic surgery, and to offer free dental inspections which will always result in future work since no one's teeth are perfect. Bottom line, if done according to my 'Dr. Brent Young Plan,' it will result in increased income."

My first thought was: *Weren't dentists already making enough money?*

He needed "zippy" slides to illustrate his talks on screen plus ads in dental journals, mailers, and a brochure. So far, he'd been gathering dentists through word of mouth (no pun intended), but wanted to expand. He was confident we were the right team to do it.

We produced the work and his practice management seminars flourished. He held sessions in Las Vegas, Hawaii, Salt Lake City, and even one in Bergen, Norway.

I asked, "Why Bergen?"

"I've always wanted to go there," he said.

Out of the dozen freelancers I interviewed, I hired one. She was a photographer whose samples showed she had a real talent in shooting people to make them look natural yet not posed, which in fact they were. She worked with us for many years, eventually starting her own successful photography studio in Las Vegas.

Her name was Charlene Garamond, and her first assignment was to shoot Dr. Brent Young behind the podium at a hotel conference room with one of my "zippy" graphic enhanced bullet point speaking topic slides behind him. Dr. Young was in his late forties with a shock of sandy-colored hair and clear blue eyes, someone who exudes easy confidence. He became a good client, eventually inviting us over to his house in Salt Lake City, where he couldn't wait to show off his 5,000 sq. ft. basement completely dedicated to an electric scale model train set.

"What do you think, guys?" he beamed, throwing a switch.

For once, John and I were speechless.

On the flight home, after much-anticipated drinks (no booze in Utah, and Dr. Young was a teetotaler who didn't even drink coffee, serving us Sanka, a decaffeinated instant powder), John said, "Hell of a long way to go and look at a damn choo-choo train."

"Yeah, but he gave us more work."

43. RIPPLE EFFECT

We had a son, Henrik, who Nika took to immediately. She was twelve years older and never put herself in the position of being the bossy sister. She treated him as an equal, and by the time he was three, begged to babysit him so we could go out on Saturday nights.

Nika was a good talker, she'd had plenty of practice with adults at the beach parties. I think, indirectly, that she elevated Hendrik's vocabulary and grasp of the world at large with her steady stream of insightful conversation. When Henrik was in 5th grade, some kids were bullying his best friend when he mentioned that he wanted to be a gardener someday. They mocked him for wanting a "dumb stupid job" and shoved him around on the playground. When class started after recess, Henrik, without anyone asking, marched to the front of the room and made somewhat of an impassioned speech defending his friend's future occupation, that the bullies had been thoughtless; and what was wrong with being a gardener anyway? There was no more bullying after Henrik's talk.

John had recovered from his divorce, met Mandy, a ten-years younger high school English teacher, and after a short engagement, got married. Together, they bought a house with a pool, and in a rare bit of socializing, invited us over to celebrate his new wife and homestead.

The house was U-shaped with the pool in the center, oddly facing the street not the backyard as might be expected. After several glasses of wine, John suggested that we should go for a swim.

Neither Stella and I had brought bathing suits, but he brushed it aside. "Who needs a suit?" he said, stripping down as Mandy quickly followed.

We complied and it seemed rather ordinary, even anticlimactic. It wasn't as if we were ready to embark on some sexual adventure of wife swapping, or were at a party with twenty other screaming, cavorting naked couples (although that could've been fun). We soon got bored paddling around, got out, dried off, dressed, and went into the house as John turned on *Saturday Night Live*. Dan Aykroyd was doing a spot-on impersonation of Julia Child in the kitchen eviscerating a chicken and soon, her fingers and hands. Blood spurted and gushed everywhere, and the audience howled with laughter. Stella looked the other way, as I pretended not to cringe.

At work, we'd reached the top of the bell curve and, while staying on the plateau for about another two years, we started to slide down. New work became harder to find, clients got wind of the 15% rebate and demanded half of it, and ad budgets were being trimmed due to a less-than-stellar economy. We were breaking even, which meant there was just enough money to pay suppliers and our secretary, but not ourselves.

Freelancers were working out of their apartments with computers, knocking out ten logos for a presentation to my hand-drawn three, and charging half the price. They didn't pay additional rent on office suites or have employees, and desktop publishing became the way to go. At some companies, secretaries often became de facto "designers" when their bosses sidestepped hiring commercial artists, having them produce ads, flyers, and announcements on their computers. Unintentionally, this produced some of the worst graphic design ever. With dozens of typefaces available at their fingertips, everyone thought that the more you used on a single-page layout, the more "creative" it would look. It was quite the opposite. In one of the commercial ad journals I subscribed to, a writer called this approach "design treason," which had the look of "paste-up ransom notes."

I had no interest in creating commercial design via a computer and soon, breaking even crashed into the red. It was time to abandon ship. John and I had been together as an incorporated partnership for seventeen years, longer than most Orange County marriages (including his). The magic was gone.

Over multiple beers at the Cock and Balls, we brainstormed - not over creating a new ad campaign, but on how we could possibly continue to earn a living. Open a bakery, surf shop, maybe a used book store. Start a strip club, and even crazier ideas.

Finally, John said, "How about a contemporary art gallery? You're sort of in the business in a way. You must know a lot of artists."

On the surface, it sounded glamorous. But what I'd read about galleries was that they were run by rich women like millionaires Peggy Guggenheim and Virginia Dwan, an heiress to the Minnesota 3M fortune, or Leo Castelli who married into wealth and got support from his father in law.

Deep pockets were required, which we didn't have; so, we brashly did it anyway. We opened a contemporary art gallery called the Garret John Gallery, using our first names. We secured just over a thousand square feet on a one-year lease downstairs in the same building we had our ad agency in. We painted the walls bone white, hired an electrician to take out the sound ceiling and install overhead track spotlights. We ripped out all the carpeting down to bare concrete floors. The space looked cool and we were ready, but we were also burning through money to get the gallery into the contemporary mode so it wouldn't appear like an office space. I was director/curator, while John handled PR and also bartended during openings.

We direct-mailed postcards I designed for each one of our openings using a three-mile radius spread out from the gallery. Our address was dead center in one of the most high-income bracket Zip Codes; next to that famous one in Beverly Hills that later had a TV series named after it.

The response was quite respectable. I doubt if we ever had less than one hundred people show up for an opening. Since Stella and I were never big on hosting parties at our home, we were now doing it by proxy at the gallery...nor did we have to worry about spilled drinks on the carpet since the gallery floors were cement. Visitors loved our free booze, hors d'oeuvres, and viewing the contemporary art. Only thing was, I didn't know 80% of them and they rarely bought art. But I enjoyed the kind of group high you get mingling with buzzed people — faces flushed, talking animatedly, while I just stood back to observe. I'd catch Stella's eyes to exchange a silent nod, as if to say: *Isn't this something*, kind of magical, really.

We found that there were devoted art groupies, people that never failed to show for an opening, who would compliment the hell out of John and I for our "dedication to exhibiting cutting-edge art in Orange County;" yet, they never spent a penny.

We did score a serious collector who almost always bought one piece per opening. But the sale came with a caveat: she wanted the invoice made out to her daughter's residence in Arizona. Why? The State has no sales tax. Her home was down south, not too far from Salt Creek, a beach I used to surf in high school. I delivered each piece she bought, marveling at her home with a circular driveway. The two-story was a kind of Norman-style castle with complicated stone work, a slate roof, topped by turrets at each end. I doubt if they were functional.

A surprise visitor was Paul Schimmel, curator at NHAM (Newport Harbor Art Museum, later to become OCMA, Orange County Museum of Art), who stood in front of one piece and said, "Too bad about this artist, I had high hopes for him, but in my opinion, he failed to live up to that promise." After Schimmel left NHAM, he would go on to a 22-year career as MOCA's (Museum of Contemporary Art) chief curator, an institution Stella and I visited many times. It's the place we saw Chris Burden's iconic motorcycle action piece *Big Wheel*.

Oddly enough, the work Schimmel more or less disparaged, I

later sold to a surgeon and his romance novelist wife. Like they say, "There's no accounting for taste."

The artists I curated into exhibitions were quite pleased to be shown in Newport Beach, even if they didn't sell. They would mention the "ripple effect" which translated into "if I don't sell here, I'll still be seen, and next time around at another gallery who knows?"

Many of the artists I chose were from LA, and none ever turned me down when I invited them. I showed brothers Guy Dill and Laddie John Dill, and Laddie's ex-wife Ann Thornycroft, Billy Al Bengston, Jim Ganzer (AKA Jimmy Z) and Robert Dowd, famous for painting American paper currency in various styles who would be charged for forgery by the FBI. The ridiculous charges were dropped when it was pretty clear that no one would ever attempt to use a 3 x 5 ft. painting on canvas as a dollar bill.

One viewer went nuts over a displayed pedestal-top ceramic sculpture. I waited for him to withdraw his checkbook, but he said, "I want my wife to see this, I'll bring her with me tomorrow."

He did, and she had one word, "Really?"

She hated it.

Our landlord came to several openings, noticed our price list could go anywhere from $1,000 to $15,000 for an individual piece, and assumed we were making money like gangbusters...and were possibly millionaires. At the end of our year lease, he offered the space at double the rent. I countered by asking for a 20% reduction because office rentals at that time were sagging with plenty of empty suites everywhere. Some of the buildings in our center were dubbed "see-throughs" since you could look right through their glass facades from one vacant end to the other. He declined my suggestion. I must say that whenever I drove past our former gallery and saw for years that it remained empty; I felt a certain amount of schadenfreude. I guess he preferred to hemorrhage monthly rent payments, rather than reduce his price. Maybe it's a tax thing?

Closing the gallery ended my business relationship with John. We now meet over coffee two or three times a year and have great conversations to disparage right-wing politics. We like to say, "If only both of us were in charge how much better things would be." Through the wonder of technology, John has set up a home recording studio to make voice-overs and podcasts. In retrospect, Garrett John Gallery of Contemporary Art had been a magical joy ride, but when it stopped, there wasn't anything to really show for it, except a new job offer.

44. THREE DEANS

The drive to my part-time teaching job at the university was a 50-mile round trip, twice a week, which involved negotiating three separate freeways. As much as I loved the university campus atmosphere, I wanted a teaching position closer to home, and that offer came from the Art Department Chair at a community college who'd attended one of our openings. Lemon Valley College was, at most, a five-minute drive from home. If my car broke down, I could probably run to class and make it in time - if I had to.

I was not hired to teach 2-D Design, or the basics of painting, or drawing, but to operate a brand-new gallery space that had just been built on campus. I guess my one-year of experience qualified me. The nice thing about being involved in exhibiting art on an academic level was I didn't have to sell anything. To make the administration realize it was a worthwhile venture for me to showcase contemporary art at their college (founded by a retired Marine Corps General) in a fairly conservative neighborhood, I had to make sure plenty of live bodies rotated through the gallery. One minor drawback, the gallery was not located in the Art Department proper but across campus in the ESL (English as Second Language) Building. There would be no art students wandering through between classes, instead I got Mid-Eastern and Asian (mostly) women poking their head in, who left nearly as quickly when they didn't see a chalkboard that translated Farsi into English.

I designed a gallery flyer which I walked through the Art Department to introduce myself to the various instructors. I suggested they could give extra credit for students coming to openings, or visiting the gallery to write a short report on whatever they saw on the walls. Unanimously, they thought it was a good idea. For the most part, every studio art class has a written assignment requirement. Instructors struggle with this because students like to moan "this isn't an English class; why do have to write something?" Generally, the assignment is to visit a museum or gallery which can mean driving to LA, something Orange County Students hate. "It's so far!" and "You have to pay to park!"

Now all they had to do was amble over to the campus gallery at leisure and write their report. I got a lot of questions, was happy to answer them - and probably, in the process, inadvertently wrote about 25% of their papers.

The university had wanted me to stay, but after driving there for five years as a student and another four as an instructor, I was tired of the on-going nine-year commute. Lon Lagerfeld wrote me a terrific letter of recommendation which I never had the opportunity to use.

Openings were well-attended: a mixture of students, their parents, faculty, and people (or civilians as we called them) from the surrounding neighborhood. The college had a good PIO (Public Information Officer) who was enthusiastic about the gallery, writing up each exhibition I presented. He was good at getting the articles printed in the local paper. He also took photos of whatever work I recommended as "the signature piece" which almost always saw print with the article.

Like at the Garrett John Gallery, I wore three hats, but fortunately it came with a salary. I was the gallery director, the curator, and the installer. When the semester ended, the department heads were pleased with what I'd accomplished and they decided to turn it into an actual teaching class, which added to my unit load. It was listed in the class schedule as Museum and Gallery Management Practices Seminar. A title my former dentist client, Dr. Young, would surely have loved.

During my tenure as head of the gallery, I went through three

Art Department deans. The first one was mostly clueless, the second possibly insane, and the third one was a wild card.

The second dean, Dr. Dennis Gerspach - who I refused to address as doctor, came into the gallery one afternoon, spun around on his tassel oxblood loafers, to rather loudly announce, "Well, if this isn't a sucking black hole."

There were about a dozen students present, some writing reports, others just gazing, and almost to the person they turned to shoot Gerspach a look that nineteen-year-olds are so good at conveying: *Who the fuck are you!*

"Dennis, why don't we step into my office and chat?" He followed me in and seated himself. I asked, "What's this all about?"

"Most art classes have around 25 students. They pay $45 dollars for the privilege, plus they buy a textbook and art supplies at our campus store. You currently have seven students, no textbook, and no supplies required." He pointed a finger at me, "You have a yearly budget of $500 dollars. That's what I mean about a black hole."

"First of all, I took the job on the condition that this was a specialty class which has the potential to be applicable for a student getting an actual job, which is taught on a Saturday, meaning enrollment would always be low. My students may become future gallery owners or museum curators who will then define the very art the public is exposed to."

Gerspach didn't comment.

"What I bring to the table..." I stopped to open a drawer and slapped a half dozen newspaper tear sheets on my desk in front of him, "...is positive publicity." Many of the articles were half-page with a photo in most cases, "above the fold."

He leaned in to pop on a pair of readers. "Hmmm...had no idea."

This, I thought, was pure bullshit. How does a dean not know there were laudatory articles in the paper about his own department?

"Is your chair comfortable?" he asked, out of nowhere.

"It's a chair."

"How would you like a new one? As of right now."

"Now?"

"Yes, follow me."

I marched behind him and he stopped in the gallery doorway to gesture at the nearest student. "I'm Dr. Gerspach, the Art Department dean, you sit behind the counter until we get back, and don't let anybody steal anything." The student made a sour face, but did it. We walked over to the Student Learning Services Center, formerly known as the Library. With a key, he opened a door to a small, empty office and there sat a plastic shrink-wrapped ergonomic chair. "It's yours," he said.

"Nice. Thanks." I started to leave the office.

"Where you going?"

"Back to the gallery."

"Fine. But take the chair with you."

"Isn't that kind of a maintenance job to deliver it?"

He smirked. "If I fill out a maintenance req, you'll be lucky to get it in ten days."

What could I do but wheel my ergonomic chair across the quad, getting strange looks from students and faculty alike. Gerspach was fired a year later for inviting female faculty into his office to demonstrate massage techniques to alleviate headaches. He was quoted as saying: "I'm good with migraines." Mysteriously, a bullet put a hole into Gerspach's office window, but it was never discovered who the perp was. One student told me, "Too bad he wasn't in his office when it happened."

My third dean, Howard Staebler, was a name dropper, who said he personally knew Wayne Thiebaud, and Anthony (Tony) Ladd, a minimalist artist highly regarded for creating illusionary works with mirrors, glass, and polished steel. He called me into his office one day to suggest, "Have you considered inviting a guest curator to produce an exhibition?" I hadn't, and figured that this was not so much a passing idea but something I had to do, most likely ASAP. "Your shows have been good, paintings on the wall, free standing sculptures, pedestal pieces, assemblages, but I think we need to be more conceptual and push the envelope a little further. Don't you?"

"By all means. Got anybody in mind that will push the conceptual envelope?"

"I do. Marlene Dumas." He fished a business card out of his blazer pocket and gave it to me. "Call her." Her card said: *Curator-at-Large*.

I did, and we met. Physically, she was scarecrow thin, vibrating with nervous energy, wore tortoiseshell glasses too big for her small face, and displayed shaggy hair that was somewhere between pink and lavender. Perhaps this was a Cyndi Lauper homage.

She caught me looking and said, "Fuchsia."

"Right on." Her concept was to invite everyone she knew to bring any clothes into the gallery they'd like to get rid of. The title of her show: *Discarded: The art of the Reusable*.

"It'll be a socially responsible exhibit that afterwards, all the cast-offs will be donated to Goodwill."

The day before the opening, her friends brought in piles of every clothing article you could imagine. With my student's help, she organized the rag bag collection into piles by color. The end result was scattered mounds of clothes about four feet high, spread across the gallery floor.

When it was completed, Marlene called Dean Staebler, who she'd known "for ages," which I seriously doubted since she appeared to be all of twenty-five years old.

My gallery students stepped aside to await the dean's opinion, flashing me a group look that strongly suggested: *Is this shit for real, or a fucking joke?*

He came in, exhibiting a broad smile. "Brilliant, Marlene. Make sure to take a lot of photos for your portfolio."

The worst part of the exhibition was the smell. I doubt if any of the clothing had been cleaned first. When the show closed, I opened both doors, brought in a shop fan, and let it blow for a whole day.

45. RENT FREE?

Other than our Europe tour which I'd planned, Stella was the master planner of our vacation getaways. One of the places she always wanted to visit was New Mexico, particularly the Georgia O'Keeffe Museum in Santa Fe. She also wanted to visit Albuquerque and Taos. She called it the New Mexico Trifecta.

She had not taken to running like I had, but enjoyed walking, particularly trails that offered scenery. She liked being in nature and we'd taken local hikes through canyons covered with huge California live oaks, and spreading sycamores. Signs were posted to be aware of mountain lions and coyotes. Coyotes were spotted loping along in the underbrush, but mountain lions remained unseen. Which is not to say the pumas weren't there. A year later, a female jogger bent over to tie her shoe, got pounced on from the rear, and was killed by massive fang bites to the back of her neck.

"You have to make yourself large," Stella said, spreading her arms, standing on tiptoes. "That scares off mountain lions. If you can jump on a rock, even better."

We saw plenty of mule deer, presumably the puma's favorite food...other than female joggers.

In Albuquerque, Stella found a hike that would take us to the top of a mountain where a Depression-era WPA stone cabin had been built, but was no longer in use. Henrik was with us, and like his sister, he was an uncomplaining avid walker. We'd dressed lightly since the starting temperature at the trailhead was in the high 80's. But as we increased our elevation, it got cooler and cooler. Also, there was dense forest growth that the sun did not penetrate. I think we may have set a hiking record to the top in our rush to stay warm. The view and air quality were spectacular, but we were shivering.

Stella suggested, "Why don't we jog back down?"

Silly question.

We didn't hike in Santa Fe, but we walked our butts off. At the Georgia O'Keeffe Museum, we lucked out. The exhibition displayed some of her most iconic paintings, installed along with the work of her one-time husband, Alfred Stieglitz, featuring his groundbreaking photography. Stella bought a poster of O'Keeffe's *Oriental Poppies*, where it now hangs in our bedroom.

The elevation at Taos is nearly 7,000 ft. and we'd planned to hike the Elliot Barker Trail which was listed as "moderate" that went for seven miles. I think we did about two miles and turned back, the thinner air kind of got to us.

The most unique aspect of Taos is the Pueblo, sometimes referred to as America's first condominiums. Built out of red adobe, some of the structures go up four stories; and that's without any re-bar. Best guess is that they were originally built around 1100, still fully inhabited to this day by about 200 Taos-native speakers who live there full-time. If there was ever a magical place, the Taos Pueblo is it.

When our daughter Nika had graduated high school, she got her first job at a donut shop, which she quit after it was robbed. She went to work at a bakery (better product, and it was nowhere near a San Diego offramp for a quick getaway) where she met an interesting boy, she was attracted to. He sat at her counter for hours sipping endless refills, writing, but he not only wrote, he also self-published little books of poetry and one-liners ("They were all Druids at the Welfare Office" and "He's got the road for a roof over his head" were two of my favorites). He rode a black Vespa and self-identified as a "Mod," a genre I thought had faded along with Carnaby Street. Evidently, there was still an active enclave of Mods in Orange County. Who knew?

His name was Stan (Stanton) Ellison, who had a pale complexion (no beach time for him), topped by a spiky head of dark hair (turned out it was a dye job), and at about six foot three made quite a contrast to Nika at five foot three. He was very soft spoken, polite, and we liked him immediately.

"So, you guys are dating?" Stella asked.

"Nah, we just hang out together."

We weren't sure if "hang out" had replaced "dating" by Gen X, but regardless, they spent a lot of time together. Stan had an entry-level job at a Metro newspaper doing page layout via a computer on the Classified Ads section.

We'd taken Nika with us to Minneapolis on two occasions, and she "loved" Grandma, the big house, Lake Harriet, and the pedestrian-friendly downtown. One visit was in the Spring, the other in the Fall, and nobody made any mention of the brutal icebox winters – the very ones Stella escaped for California.

During dinner with Stan and Nika, I was listening to Stan rationalize that he didn't think "it was impossible for a parallel universe to exist; after all, in this infinite space continuum why should it only be us? And wasn't string theory super interesting how it describes-"

Nika gave Stan a tender smile, clasped his hand, to state matter of fact, "We have an announcement."

Before either Stella or I could reply, both of us thinking this was the big one. Marriage, surely?

"First of all, don't you guys think it's kind of boring around here?" When we didn't comment, Nika continued, "We're moving to Minneapolis. Isn't that cool?"

Yes, soon enough it really will be cool, I wanted to say.

"Aw," Henrik said, "my sister's ditching me."

"I'll write."

Their plan was to arrive on Grandma's doorstep, and offer to pay whatever rent she wanted for a room. It didn't quite work out that way. Grandma greeted them warmly, and served tuna fish sandwiches with a cucumber salad for lunch when Stan popped the rent question.

"Oh, no dear, I couldn't accept that," she said.

Stan brightened and had misunderstood that Nika's sweet Grandma was offering a rent-free stay. "You mean you won't take any rent?"

"No, I mean I can't have an unmarried couple sleeping under my roof."

I doubt if either Nika or Stan had taken Grandma's Lutheran protocol into consideration. So be it. They would have to find their little bit of magic elsewhere. And they did.

46. PERMANENT COLLECTION

Stella and I went to a one-man exhibition of Tony Ladd's work at a private college. We liked his work, but hadn't seen much of it in nearly a decade and were curious how he'd evolved. Spanning one whole gallery wall was a series of concept sketches on graph paper mounted with push pins. I liked the informal presentation, almost as if the viewer had stepped into the artist's studio.

This show was devoid of his sculpture to strictly focus on his painting. He'd created a series of asymmetrical-shaped paintings that bulged outwards from the wall that were painted in monochromatic, almost industrial, colors.

Ladd, about ten years older than I, wore a ponytail and a Van Dyke going gray. He was casually dressed in jeans, a black denim shirt, running shoes, and was surrounded by a group of about a dozen well-wishers, some offering the catalog for his autograph. On the spur of the moment, I decided to make a rather brash move that I'd never considered, and wouldn't do again.

"Give me a couple of minutes," I told Stella.

I inserted myself right into Ladd's crowd, ignored everyone, and grabbed his hand, shaking it briskly. "Tony, so good to see you. Love your new work. Howard Staebler couldn't make it and asked me to say hello."

"Howard Stable...?"

He seemed befuddled, like he'd never heard the name. "Right, Howard Staebler, he's the art department dean where I teach at

Lemon Valley College." Had Howard made it up, and really didn't know the artist?

"Anyway, my wife and I are big admirers. That's her right over there." I'd heard that Tony was a bit of a lady's man, and when Stella waved a winsome smile, he broke into an appreciative grin. "The pinned paperworks, that's a great presentation."

"My idea, actually. Someone give...what's your name?"

"Garrett DeWalt."

He snapped his fingers. "Someone give Mr. DeWalt a catalog so I can autograph it for him."

A young woman quickly ran off, returned with his catalog, and Tony signed it with a flourish. "Here you go. Are you an artist?"

"Yes."

"Great. Very nice talking to you, say hi to...Grabber...whatshis-name."

"Howard Staebler. Will do. Take care, Tony."

I left his circle where I was immediately approached by a rather nondescript person who wore a long-sleeved, untucked wrinkled shirt, apparently a new style. Barely in his thirties, he was already suffering male pattern baldness. It reminded me of an old Bob Hope joke: *The guy wore a crew cut and most of the crew had bailed out.*

"Hi, I'm Michael Leigh Davis."

"Always go by three names?"

"There's another curator whose name is Michael Davis, so I use all three to cut any confusion. Anyway, I'm the curator here. So, I see you personally know Tony Ladd."

"Yes, Tony, great guy." My spontaneous ruse had evidently impressed Michael Leigh Davis, who was the gallery's curator! I'd been prepared to ignore him, but now it was time to play nice. "I'm Garrett DeWalt, the curator at Lemon Valley College. I exhibit my paintings at LACMA." I didn't mention it was at the Art Rental and Sales Gallery, leaving it at that.

"LACMA," He nodded thoughtfully. "Well, actually we have a permanent collection of contemporary art here on campus. I'd love to include you in. Interested?"

Say no more.

Tony Ladd, master of illusion, who in the early part of his career performed magic tricks at art happenings, now through my subterfuge had unwittingly introduced me into a significant permanent collection at a very expensive private college. Months later, I got an RSVP invitation to the university's book release party of their published, full-color permanent collection in glossy hardback.

I had my own page.

That evening, we got a phone call from Nika saying she'd landed a job as 'Girl Friday' to the Assistant District Attorney of Hennepin County in Minneapolis. How she aced that interview is beyond me, because this is a girl whose resumé consisted of: High School Graduate, Donut Shop, Bakery.

"How about Stan?" I asked.

"He got a job at a copy center, and loves it."

They would last through two winters until the snow, ice, and slush got to be overwhelming, and returned to sunny Southern California. It had been magical while it lasted. But they still thought our well-ordered suburban neighborhood, with its surrounding area was "too beige - too boring," and moved into an upper story four-plex in Long Beach, close to Downtown on Broadway plus whatever excitements that city offered (which, in fact, were many).

"The most unusual thing I did at the DA's office," Nika once said, "was to deliver a subpoena to a man living under a bridge."

"Did he accept it?"

"You bet."

47. BUYING ART

I attended the private university book release soiree of their permanent collection, which was a pretty swank affair with black-tie waitstaff and enough champagne to keep everyone happy. Artists in attendance wore little pin-on plastic badges identifying us to the crowd who weren't artists. Actually, it was pretty easy to spot who was and wasn't. Wear a suit, you're not an artist.

A woman in stylish ripped jeans and a purple Prince T-shirt rushed forward, nearly spilling her flute. She grabbed my arm, kissed both cheeks, gushing, "You practically rescued my career, thank god."

Her artist tag said Lisa Baker. I remembered curating her into my inaugural exhibition at Garrett John Gallery. "Thanks, but as I recall, none of your work sold."

She shook her head. "No matter. Right after that, I was picked up by a gallery in Santa Monica for a three-person group show, where I sold two pieces. I've been doing pretty well since."

"Ah, the ripple effect."

"Yes, exactly. I see your painting in the book. Cool. Had no idea you were an artist. No more gallery director?"

"No, that was just a hobby." (By definition, an activity you like doing without getting paid.)

Lisa emptied her flute and flagged a waiter over for more. "You know, I still have the invitation poster you designed, with my name listed on top over all the other artists. I got some shit from the guys over that."

"Well, just give them shit back. You deserved to be on top." I didn't tell her the listing was alphabetical, B as in Baker.

I sipped my champagne and milled about; the heavy book proudly clutched in one hand. Searching through the crowd of identified artists, I didn't know anyone other than Lisa. A man in a tan blazer but no tie, approached, and stared at my ID. He introduced himself as Isaac Gundersen, Art Department Chair at Bristol College.

"I read your bio; that you're local, once were an art director of an ad agency you co-founded, ran your own gallery, taught 2-D Design at university, are affiliated with LACMA's ARS Gallery, and here you are curated into this very impressive permanent collection at a prestigious college. Congratulations."

I felt like casually blowing it off as "no big deal," but it was.

"I'd like to offer you a job."

I took a moment to consider it. "Okay...thanks. What position are you offering?"

"Positions, as in plural. Two actually. One Basic Drawing, the other Art Theory."

"Art Theory, what's that about?"

He patted my back. "Easy money. You'll have a class textbook, but you can cherry pick the parts you like. I mean the damn thing is like 400-plus pages, no way an instructor can cover the whole thing in one semester." He chuckled, "Hell, I never did. You can pretty much ignore prehistoric art, Mesopotamia, Egypt, and touch on the Greco-Roman Empire as it relates to the Renaissance. Sometimes I'd start the class with Andy Warhol's *Marilyn Monroe* because of her instant recognizability."

"Are you saying I don't have to teach the different art periods chronologically?"

"Exactly. Hop, skip around, keep it fresh. Interested?'

"Keep talking."

"Come see me tomorrow, I'll explain and sign you up for the next semester. Now, autograph your page for me."

I guess this was another example of the ripple effect.

Gundersen never bothered to ask whether I wanted the job.

But I did want it, and quit at Lemon Valley College at semester's end when Staebler foisted another one of his young, female protégés "curator-at-large" on me who wanted to do something with coat hangers suspended from the ceiling. I wished her luck.

Before I walked out of his office, I said, "I talked to Tony Ladd the other day, and he says you're welcome to drop by his studio, anytime."

Right then and there, judging by his befuddled expression, I knew that Staebler did not know Tony.

"Don't forget, now."

Stella decided she needed to get a job since my part-time college gallery class wasn't exactly earning big bucks, and even with supplemental ARS Gallery income, we needed more. A mortgage hangs over you like a dark cloud. It's not like you can move into a cheaper apartment. She signed up for a paid two-week teller-training course through Bank of America and graduated as a full-time merchandising teller.

When she sought the job, her criteria were:

1. It has to be clean
2. Have all major holidays off
3. Has to come with health benefits and retirement
4. And not to put too fine a point on it — have banker's hours

We both fell into our new job routines with ease. Stella said that even though it was "a little scary," she did enjoy the responsibility of making huge cash deposits brought in by merchants and corporations. "Everyone really treats me very nicely."

At Bristol College, I especially liked lecturing in an auditorium with sloped seating backed by a movie-size screen for projecting slides. In my gallery class at Lemon Valley College, last count I had eight students, here I had eighty-seven. Since the gallery at Irvine was cross campus from the art department, I always felt a little estranged, and never got to know the other art faculty all that well.

I came to be pretty good friends with Isaac Gunderson, and he invited us over to his house for "a spot of wine." His home was a spreading Craftsman-style on a quiet Huntington Beach cul-de-sac. The minute we stepped inside it was like entering a house-sized museum of California contemporary art. Almost from floor to ceiling hung prime examples of art, which made me wonder at what stage of collecting Isaac was at. It's been said that the true collector will fill his house until there's no wall space left, then goes out to secure a storage unit, and fills that. In the end, the collection can go to offspring or get donated to a museum.

A young man, in a Gold's Gym T-shirt introduced as Barney, filled our glasses with wine from a cardboard box, a first for us.

"Really comes in handy for traveling," Isaac said. "Three of these neatly fit into a suitcase, and I'm ready to go. You should have seen the French airport inspector's expression when he looked into my suitcase. 'Mon dieu! Wine in a box!'"

"Did you offer him any?" Stella asked.

Isaac broke into a huge grin. "Of course. Best way to get through customs."

Barney brought us a tray of hors d'oeuvres, was thanked by Isaac, and he disappeared upstairs. We got to talking about our VW Bus trip through Europe and all the great museums we visited, when Isaac asked, "Don't suppose you ever went to Russia and toured the Hermitage?"

"Maybe on our next trip," Stella said.

"By all means do." Isaac refilled his glass with more wine from the little spigot attached to the bottom of the box. "When I was at the Hermitage, the security was unbelievably lax; lax as in almost negligent. There was only this one babushka guarding a whole huge gallery of Impressionist, Post-Impressionist, and Fauve art. She was fast asleep on a little stool. Under Communism, everyone is guaranteed a job for life. That was hers. Believe me," he laughed, "I could very easily have stolen a Matisse or two."

"And the Russians would've never known you took it," Stella said.

"True, oh so true," Isaac nodded wistfully, maybe wishing he should've.

Obviously, Isaac wasn't married, presumably had no kids, so I felt compelled to ask. I motioned at all the spectacular art on the walls. "Who gets this when you're-"

"Gone?" he interrupted with a grin. "Well, no one in my immediate or extended family. I'll tell you why."

The story was that he'd started buying California artists — almost wholly LA-based — when he got his first teaching job. His salary was low, but so were art prices for this new crop of LA artists he was devoted to. Many of these artists were happy enough to make a sale, they'd give him an additional piece for free. As the years progressed and his salary increased, so did the art market and he kept buying. He'd put pieces up for auction, take the profit, to buy a higher-priced work.

"My parents, especially my older brother, teased me mercilessly that I was throwing money away on weird art no one was interested in. I could get better stuff at a swap meet, my brother once claimed. Anyway, I had an appraiser come out to view my collection not too long ago. He said it was worth between 1.5 to 2 million. A small article appeared in the paper about the worth of my 'Isaac Gundersen collection,' and I started getting phone calls from relatives I had never heard of. Even one from Denmark. My brother pleaded to get a few pieces...hah! Screw them all. When I leave this planet, it's going to LACMA."

Unfortunately, Isaac would leave all too soon. Six years later, he died and although I never heard from *what*, it was whispered that it was HIV-related.

I inherited his office.

48. ON THE CARPET

When you're an artist, you never know how much of your creative DNA will be passed into your children. Other than Nika's painting spree to make posters to get elected as the 6th grade school president, she had not followed up on any more painting. In Minneapolis, she'd bought a camera and taken lots of photos. She put together several mini-albums of her work, and my impression was that she had a great natural eye for color, composition, and slightly off-kilter framing to give the work the appropriate contemporary edge.

Now living in Long Beach, she got a job at a big, centrally-located camera shop, which she really liked, where she also managed to pick up technical tips from the staff. But months later she felt something was "emotionally missing." She found the answer one day, posted in a local free weekly. She applied for a position at the downtown Mental Health Wellness Center. Her resumé was obviously still slim, with no real background or education in the mental health field. However, Nika has the magical ability to easily radiate cheerful self-confidence, always a winning attribute when job seeking. She knows how to make a great first impression.

Her interviewer noted Nika's two years working in a big city DA's office as "a positive step in negotiating red tape." She went on to say, "You know, I've always admired attitude over aptitude, and you have that aplenty. What I want is a one-page letter explaining why you want this job."

Never at a loss for words, written or spoken, she wrote a heartfelt letter that landed her a position as an intake counselor. Nika has always had a soft spot for the dispossessed, never failing to give a homeless person a handout. Now, she'd be on the front lines at a clinic, dealing with every kind of street person you can imagine. Tweakers, acid heads, self-medicators, alcoholics, paranoids, and just plain general whack jobs. Nika would deal with a host of their problems as an advocate, without ever being judgmental.

While live-in boyfriend Stan was doing classified-page lay-outs for the city's main metro paper, he was also doing small adds on the side for pot shops. He liked to partake, happily doing the work as trade out for product.

Stella and I have never done much weed, but on occasion friends would kind of gently persuade us to join in.

In our first apartment, after we returned from my army jaunt in Alexandria, we invited Roger (a surfing buddy) and his girl, Roxie, over. He brought a greenish-glass bowl-shaped object with about a foot-long tube on top that came with four attached narrow hoses. "You guys ever tried one of these?" Roger said. "It's a hookah."

"Nope," we both said.

"It's, like, crazy fun."

Without going into a lot of detail, we got appropriately buzzed. Roxie took it upon herself to go to the Market Basket and buy a chocolate cake which we devoured by hand because Roger said, "It's so much fucking tastier this way."

Since our living room was bare cracked linoleum, one of our first purchases to cover up as much floor as possible was an eight by ten-foot Persian carpet bought at the Orange County Swap Meet. (If you remember, we left behind our oval braided carpet - with the burn holes - in Alexandria.) Now, the four of us were flaked out on our backs while listening to the Beatles *Strawberry Fields*, group singing, "...nothing is real and nothing to get hung about..."

Roger made the astute observation that cottage-cheese sound ceilings "suck and are disgusting to look at," so we rolled over onto our stomachs.

Next morning, Stella came out of the bathroom, shooting me a quizzical glance as she spotted me on hands and knees on the Persian carpet. "Looking for leftover chocolate crumbs?"

"I'm looking for John Kennedy."

"Sorry?"

"Right about here," I said sweeping my hand over a patch. "Last night, I swear I saw Jack in the weave of this abstract floral patterning. He had his arms across his bare chest. But now I can't find him."

"Pity. I'm going to make breakfast. I'll call when it's ready."

I never did relocate Jack. We still have the carpet, and sometimes I take a minute or so to look. I know he's in there somewhere.

For Nika and Stan, life in Long Beach was filled with events like street art fairs, poetry readings, happenings, and sound artist performers who organized installations that spanned block after block. There was even a gowned opera singer in a hotel lobby. But one event they could do without was the annual Long Beach Grand Prix, an Indy street-circuit car race. They were close enough to the course that they kept the windows shut for the weekend because the engine roar from the high-performance cars made conversation impossible.

Nika got the idea to leave Long Beach entirely on Grand Prix weekends and they started camping in Joshua Tree. Here, they were treated to solitude in possibly the most surreal of California landscapes, composed of strange rock formations that could easily have been sculpted by alien forces. The spindly Joshua Trees are found nowhere else on the planet, serving as an iconic symbol for the whole valley. The clear night sky is void of inner-city light pollution, perfect for star gazing. "You can see the Milky Way," Stan said, with an eye out for potential UFOs. (He's a Sci-Fi buff.) It was the anti-Long Beach environment. After multiple camping trips over the years, they moved to Joshua Tree.

49. TELLERS

S tella and I received news we hoped never to get. Merger mania had set into the corporate financial landscape and Bank of America bought Security Pacific. Jobs would have to be consolidated or closed down. Stella was in her 7th year as a merchandising teller, but her SecPac counterpart had been at it for eleven years, and she got the job. Stella was left with a choice, go part-time, or quit.

She stayed with Bank of America for another year, but preferred full-time. She went to another bank, but just as a regular teller. "It's funny," she said, "in high school, I really didn't like math, yet I love my job as a teller, and I'm really good at it."

In all her years as a teller, she was never "under one penny or over one penny;" both cases being equally bad when you close for the day and have to "balance."

However, she was robbed twice. First time it happened, she froze and the robber quietly scooted over to the next teller, where he absconded with $850 dollars. When interviewed by the FBI, she reported that he had an Australian accent, but she had enough presence of mind and talent to draw a picture of his gun which he had pretty much stuck in her face. Turned out it was a Glock, and the perp was an Australian. He was caught only days later, readily confessing he hadn't been able to find a job, using his last bit of cash to purchase the Glock.

Second time, it was a jogger in a peach-colored velour tracksuit (Stella called it "hideous") with a ball cap pulled low. She didn't freeze up, this time following protocol by handing him the money with the special packet, then covertly pressed the button that alerts police. He shoved the money into a paper bag down his pants and casually walked out. Even though tellers or administrative staff may be aware of what just happened, the procedure is to do nothing. In other words, let the person have an exit strategy to avoid any threat of violence so no potential harm comes to any customers. The jogging robber was discovered about a mile away between oleander bushes by a gardener who heard him writhing in pain. He was covered in the exploded purple dye, screaming over and over, "Help! My balls are on fire!"

Bank officers jokingly call a robbery "an unauthorized withdrawal."

My not-so-good-news came from ARS Gallery at LACMA via a phone call.

"We're sorry to inform you, but ARS is closing shop. We'll notify you at the end of the month if you have any pieces outstanding for pick up."

That was it. The gallery had been my magical entry ticket into freely roaming the museum at will, but also exposing my work to LA. I'd had sales to major law firms, a hospital, a TV series production firm, a real estate agency, and to individual collectors.

Upper management at the museum wanted a near complete redo of its campus. The footprint of the three original buildings, designed by William Pereira in 1965, was now considered outdated. (Imagine a museum in Europe designated as "old," built in 1965.) At the time, Pereira's work was hailed as "futuristic," and he even made the cover of Time magazine, his determined visage looking ready for Mt. Rushmore. The ARS Gallery was in one of those three buildings which was slated to be demolished. I'd lost my own small footprint in LA's artworld due to progress, and unlike Stella, I had no Plan B.

Through a former connection, Nika hooked me up with a small Long Beach gallery where I was invited into a group show. One of my two pieces sold, and the owner was very enthusiastic about the work, but sales in ensuing months dribbled to near zero and she shut the operation down. Statistically, about 90% of start-up galleries fail in the first two years. And I can attest to that.

Nika and Stan were Henry Miller fans, and before they'd become mesmerized by Joshua Tree's mystical beauty, they'd camped around Big Sur, the one-time home of Henry Miller. They'd visited the Henry Miller Memorial Library where you don't check-out books, you *buy* them. (In his later years, Miller was known to play Ping Pong with naked ladies - a bit like Duchamp playing chess with an unclothed Eve Babitz.) While they still lived in Long Beach, Nika and Stan decided to get married, choosing Big Sur as their place to tie the knot. The exact spot they wanted to do this, was under the famous Bixby Creek Bridge — and if you've ever seen a TV car commercial, then you've seen the amazingly photogenic, open-spandrel arch bridge. Stella and I had driven over it a few times on the way to San Francisco or Monterey, but had never taken the ramp to go below. And now, here we were. The location for them was an homage to Miller and a reminder of their previous camping.

Neither Nika or Stan attended a church, nor did she did want a stranger to perform their marriage (as opposed to the stranger who performed ours), so Stan's father was chosen. He was a pastor at a non-denominational Christian church that he'd founded. The six of us (including Stan's mother Bessie) stood in the chill of a Pacific breeze, as Pastor Clement performed the marriage ceremony. They were now Mr. and Mrs., and surely would be welcome to spend the night under Grandma's roof.

Nika likes to put meaning into events (like choosing Big Sur) and she'd picked a Monday to get married because that was the very day she'd met Stan. I called the art secretary at Bristol college to have her cancel my two Monday classes.

"Garrett, what's the occasion?"

"Daughter is getting married."

"On a Monday?"

"That's what I said."

Retiring after teaching for nineteen years at Bristol College, that particular Monday was the only "sick day" I ever took.

Not by choice, Stella would once again move to another bank. One morning, she found her bank's parking lot filled with Federal agents. Inexplicably, one was guarding the Dumpster by the side of the building.

"What's going on?" she asked.

"Are you an employee?'

She showed her ID badge. "Yes."

"Go inside and pick up an empty cardboard box to fill with your belongings. We are confiscating everything that is worth more than $25 to sell at auction. If it's under, it goes into the trash and gets locked up. This bank is now out of business."

"But why?"

"Your bosses set up a dummy corporation to buy non-existent computers and put the cash into their pockets. Lots of it. Evidently, they didn't feel they were rich enough."

"I had no idea."

"Good answer," he smiled thinly. "Ever been upstairs in the corporate offices?"

"Nope."

"They have a sauna, a jacuzzi, with obscene amounts of expensive catered food."

"And we got Pogen's." When Stella exited twenty minutes later, she held up a potted plant. "Is this less than twenty-five bucks, or will you auction it off?"

"Take it, lady," the agent said. "By the way, what kind of plant is that?"

"A wandering Jew."

"For good reason, I suppose."

Stella never looked back, applied to her third bank, got the job, and stayed with them until retirement. Fred, the branch president, and his wife, Cyd, hosted an employee Christmas party annually at his sumptuous community gate-guarded home, which we always attended. One evening after several Sierra Nevada Celebration Ales, Stella studied her fellow workers.

"You know what would make a great TV sitcom? I'd call it *Tellers*."

"Go on."

"Every teller has a different personality; the violin-playing gay guy, the love-struck Pakistani girl, the old lady that should've retired years ago, the easy going Latino, and yours truly. For conflict, there are the officers making ridiculous demands on us while scrolling through their smartphones at selfies taken at Curacao, or some other tropical paradise, us teller peons could never afford. And then there are the customers." She took a long swallow of beer. "Oh, boy, the customers, what a bunch they are. When I asked this one overly-Botoxed bleach blonde, Corona del Mar woman in her Lululemon pants for her ID, she said, 'Do you know who I am?'"

"It'll be a hit series." I cupped my ear. "Just listen to that uproarious laugh track."

And that's as far as we ever took it. But…if anyone out there in the TV business is looking for an original, scripted three-camera sitcom, Stella has over twenty years of really good material.

50. A GOOD RUN

B y my calculation, the biggest wave I ever caught was a ten-footer on the South side of the Huntington Pier, riding my Jacks bodyboard. Jacks surf shop is directly across PCH from the start of the pier and also a Frisbee toss away from where the Golden Bear used to be. It gave the hair-raising event a kind of symbolic stature. I say "hair-raising" because when I took off, facing those larger than life pier pilings, I thought, *this could be it.* Somehow, I managed to complete the wave, successfully pull out, and not get slammed into those threatening, mussel encrusted cement pilings.

The bodyboard did not come with a leash, and it was strictly a white-knuckle grip to hold on, tumbling through the soup without losing it. If I lost my hold, I'd have to go for a protracted swim to retrieve it. Chasing after a board was an unproductive energy user. One day as I came home from a day in the surf, what should I see but a sleek, tri-fin bodyboard with a leash leaning against our red Adirondack (knock-off) plastic chair on the front patio.

"Like it?" Stella said through the open kitchen window.

"Like it? No. I love it!"

"I got it at a garage sale around the corner."

As much as I liked my Jacks bodyboard, I immediately stowed it into the rafters of my studio. That tri-fin Stella bought for me was the best ever. Magical.

I started surfing when I was 15 and stopped when I was 55. That's forty years of sun exposure without using sunblock, but no one told us about the ramifications down the road. Stella admitted that she and her girlfriends applied baby oil at Lake Harriet to speed up the tanning process. Like me, she's also made a few visits to the dermatologist.

For Stella's 60th birthday I bought her a battery-assist bike. Irvine has more bike trails than any other city in Orange county. She loved the bike, taking off for an hour at a time to explore the different trails. Flipping on the battery mode, she could pedal uphill as easily as if she was going downhill. "It's like having a super power," she said.

Sometimes, I'll catch a glimpse of my tri-fin in the rafters, balanced on top of the Jacks board and wistfully think: *Whatever happened to those days?* Occasionally, the leash mysteriously dislodges itself, dangles down, and whispers to me: *Garrett, why did you quit me? You had plenty of good years left.*

I'm joking. But it does manage to dangle down on its own accord.

Recently one of the all-time surfing greats, Mike Doyle, died at age 78.

I thought, *no way dude, that's way too fucking early.*

My running "career" as I jokingly call it, ended on an entirely different note. I did not stop voluntarily. Jogging around the very lake that my one-time client had designed, a kid on a bike slammed into my left leg, hard. I flew over his handlebars and crashed onto the paved path on my left side, scraping the skin off my wrist and elbow. There was a lot of blood which I wiped at with my bandana. The pain was intense. I looked up at the kid, who shrugged and, without apology, rode off. (Evidently, his bike was undamaged.) I lay there for a minute, and rolled over onto the grass to figure my next step, so to speak. I realized, right then and there, I'd never run again. My Achilles tendon felt weirdly jacked out of shape, forcing me to hobble the remaining two miles home.

Stella saw the outward damage, helped me to the bathroom, cleaned and liberally dosed me with Neosporin, patched bandages wherever she could. Then. she gave me the first pain-relief pill I'd ever taken. I went straight to bed and stayed there for three days.

Stella provided me with an empty orange juice bottle to relieve my-self because the trip to the bathroom would have been too painfully difficult.

Days later, I pulled the sheets back to inspect myself and I no-ticed a purple bruise the size of a watermelon on my right hip. I guess I was fortunate that nothing broke.

"From now on, I'm joining the ranks of walkers," I said.

Stella kissed me. "Well, you had a good run."

In all, I ran over 25,000 miles.

People recognize me in the neighborhood since I've been run-ning here for decades. Now, they stop me. "Why are you walking? What's wrong? You're limping." (Yes, I have a permanent limp.) I hadn't realized I was such a recognizable figure.

I feel like I should make a tape recording that explains how the unapologetic pre-teen smashed me with his bike and bashed my Achilles tendon, so I wouldn't have to repeat it to everyone that stops to inquire. A guy with one great silver mustache, I regularly see walking, noticed I wasn't running, said rhetorically, "It's not the same is it?"

But what really pisses me off as an ex-runner, is that people are walking faster than I am.

I'm still painting and although I didn't have a Plan B when the ARS Gallery closed, one was thrown into my lap. Two women who'd worked at the gallery, which I only knew in passing, had teamed up to operate their own gallery — but not as a "brick and mortar" enterprise. They'd chosen me as one of their "favorites," among 25 other artists. I was asked to send JPEGs of 10 works which they'd download on their laptop to make direct client presentations. They didn't need to bother with storage space or staffing, and all that came with the operation of running a gallery.

One partner, Mildred, lived in Westwood, an easy trip on the 405 freeway with a single turn-off, while the other one, Cate, lives in Calabasas, a trickier multi-freeway, two-hour jaunt. As we did at the ARS Gallery, artists delivered their own work, while the rest was taken care of by a professional installer.

I like the two women; they're hip and responsive to all kinds of contemporary art. They are also very good at what they do. Galleries take a 50% bite out of sales, but they keep it at 35%. I mostly work with Cate who sports short, fashionable hairdos, and is always enjoyable to talk to. Recently when Southern California seemed to be on fire, she and her husband had to vacate their Calabasas home. The only damage came as Cate, in a hurry to get out, accidentally dropped a laptop on the top of her bare foot. She showed me a scar as evidence. I didn't want to play the "I've got even a better story" gambit, and refrained from mentioning my smashed leg. Surprisingly, she's never asked me why I limp. Maybe it's just good upbringing mixed with a dash of discretion on her part.

LACMA, in the meanwhile, had made an open call for architectural submissions to create a new museum from the ground up. Proposals arrived from all over the globe. The museum mounted an exhibition of the different architects' concepts, which included spectacular renderings, blueprints, scale models, computerized simulations, and aerial views. All were consequently rejected.

After several years of going through the selection process, Swiss architect Peter Zumthor was the museum's final choice. His proposal was to build a rambling, amoeba-shaped black-roofed building that would sprawl across the property, including a small section to span Wilshire Blvd. The black color and shape were his concept of a visual reminder of LACMA's proximity to its equally-famous neighbor, the LA Tar Pits - known for its life-size fiberglass casts of a mammoth family. Easily seen from Wilshire Blvd., mama mammoth and baby mammoth stand in shock at the pit's dirt edge as they watch papa mammoth slowly sink into the tar ooze, unable to escape. 3.5 million fossils from 600 species have been recovered from the tar.

The public's immediate reaction blasted the Swiss architect for being out of touch with LA's near year-round unrelenting sunshine. "A black building, what the fuck's he thinking?" So, he changed it to beige.

The LA Times art and architectural critics didn't go for the design (beige or not), and neither did I. The two independently wrote detailed articles why they considered Zumthor's concept wrong for the site. One even pointed out that the Zumthor plan would *decrease* the museum's size by 50,000 sq. feet! Public comments tagged the organic shaped design "a coffee table," "a Palm Springs Motel," and a roadside "Toll Plaza." In order for city funding to be approved ($117 million in taxpayers funds), the Zumthor proposal was brought before the County Board of Supervisors (known as the Supes), and guess who liked it? Brad Pitt and Diane Keaton, who appeared in person to glowingly speak up for it.

This being LA, guess who the council listened to? Highly qualified and respected art and architectural experts, or two actors? With their blessing, Zumthor's proposal got the Supes whole-hearted approval.

51. JOSHUA TREE

Nika has always been anti-beige, transforming every place she and Stan have rented into a warm, inviting, and colorful home. And, always accomplished it on a limited budget. She could convert an army tent into a place you'd want to live.

Their home in Joshua Tree is situated on a slight rise, giving an unobstructed view down across the basin to Highway 62 that will take you to Arizona, where, for some reason, gasoline is always cheaper. Regular patio visitors include: coyotes, roadrunners, tortoises, tarantulas, quail, jackrabbits, doves, and a solitary rattlesnake. They didn't kill it, but called in a rattlesnake wrangler who safely bagged it to return the rattler to a more isolated stretch of desert.

Joshua Trees are protected by law. If you buy a piece of empty property, the architect will have to design the house around the Joshuas, they cannot be cut down. We've watched bulldozers grade a new lot, artfully going around the trees without doing any damage.

Nika found a comparable job as she had in Long Beach, working at a mental health facility, while Stan has decided to go totally freelance. His specialty is book design. It's amazing how many people want to be self-published, particularly the memoir. Maybe it's a way of setting the record straight in the author's mind. Stan translates the written into the graphic. When his design is completed, the very satisfied future-author not only gets a book, but a work of art. And I speak from experience as he's designed two of my books. Not only that, Stan occupies a rather unique position in publishing, he's also a novelist who designs his own books! How many authors can lay claim to that?

When Stella and I visit, they take us to all their favorite haunts. We drink at the Joshua Tree Saloon, where they hold court every Friday after work with a rotating group of like-minded locals. (Musicians, artists, poets, writers, and a few off-the-grid renegades.) A must stop-off place for anyone is Pioneertown's Pappy and Harriet's. Even Sir Paul McCartney's been there — to perform that is. Beer is served in Mason jars.

Pioneertown was built in the 1940's as an 1880's-style Western film set, and a host of movies were shot there including *Annie Oakley* and *Judge Roy Bean*.

But, two of the more unusual desert venues are the Integraton and Noah Purifoy's outdoor assemblage sculptures. We went to the Integraton for its famous sound bath rejuvenation, where you rest supine on Mexican blankets under the dome as live quartz crystal bowls are played that subtly thrum through your brain. The building was designed by George Van Tassel, a devoted ufologist. According to the posted notices, the wooden domed space offers perfect acoustical vibrations. Words can't quite describe it. You have to go in person, hear, absorb, and appreciate the full aural experience.

Noah Purifoy is an African American artist who installed over 100 assemblage sculptures over a ten-acre site. Everything is some kind of cast-off, from bicycles to washing machines, furniture, televisions, truck tires, and a lot of detritus that's hard to identify under the baking desert heat. Hint: bring sunblock.

But of all the places to hang out, we love being in their home the best. We enjoy each other's company immensely, like and dislike the same politicians, discuss art, novels, museum exhibits, and movies while drinking IPAs. As Stan shows me his latest book design project(s) on screen (currently an NFL cheerleader's memoir), Nika chatters away about her diverse array of clientele at the mental health center. One difference between Long Beach and Joshua Tree, is that there are far less homeless in Joshua. Managing a life on the streets of Long Beach with its basic temperate climate is one thing, but sleeping outdoors in the desert which is too hot in summer and too cold in winter is life threatening. American Indians have a word for those who don't survive a winter's night outside: Popsicles.

52. DON'T CRY

Henrik graduated with a BA in graphic design, from the same Cal State University where I had taught. He bounced around for a few years at different design jobs, but really didn't care for any of them. What he really liked was his home environment, the house he was born in. Instead of charging him rent, we feel we should pay him for taking care of us. He cooks all dinners, and basically maintains the house. I think of him as our primary caregiver, but he probably wouldn't like me saying that. For us, he keeps it all together.

Also, he's an invaluable help in documenting my paintings. He photographs them, downloads and makes color corrections, removes the background, then labels them by title, medium, and year completed. These have become a ready JPEG file for me to send to interested clients. When I mistakenly send copy or other info into the ether, he's my computer tech-support guru who can magically retrieve it. Don't ask me how.

Both of us retired years ago, but I still keep as active as possible in local art events. I exhibit regularly in the Long Beach Art Museum Biennial Auction, which presents a great opening night with a jazz trio. Cate also keeps me busy with whatever she has in store for me.

Marco Phillips, the art gallery director (and future department chair) at Bristol College has done his best to call me back (twice) after I retired to try and convince me to teach again, but I've declined. I really like my free time so I can spend more hours devoted to the studio. He did, however, curate me into a one-person exhibition at a street front gallery in downtown Santa Ana, that the college manages. The opening was held on what is called "First Saturday of the Month," when surrounding art galleries get into the act. The event features street musicians, art demonstrations, and outdoor booths selling everything from Frida Kahlo T-shirts to tacos. I'd say about 100 people came through the gallery first night which resulted in five sales, including my largest-ever work (10 x 8 ft.) and my smallest at 9 x 12 inches.

About five years ago, Stella started feeling poorly, an unusual condition for my active lifelong partner. Her back ached to the point where she had to lay down, barely being able to move. Her doctor thought it might be the onset of rheumatoid arthritis and recommended an epidural for pain relief, but it didn't work. Sometimes several shots are needed to be effective he said, but when we read about a 35-year-old woman getting paralyzed from the waist down after her first shot, she declined the second procedure.

His next analysis was that it might be psychosomatic. As women age, he said, and find they can no longer be as active as they once were, they become depressed, which can affect their overall well-being. He suggested going to a psychiatrist.

I disagreed, but I'm not a doctor. My take, we all become depressed about our aging bodies, but that's not quite the same as a clinical depression. Getting my leg smashed was no picnic, and it did depress me, but I never felt the need to talk to a professional about it. Stella went three times and said it was a waste of time. I agreed.

One night, Stella felt particularly bad, so we took her to the ER. She was thoroughly checked and all vital signs were as normal as could be. Their solution was to give her some high-dose pain pills.

We tried different doctors to find what her condition might be. Finally, through a recommendation, we went to a highly regarded neurologist when Stella was at her lowest ebb. She could barely walk, had to hold on to my arm for support. When she sat opposite the neurologist, her chin nearly sagged to her chest.

"Can I see your driver's license?" he asked.

A bit flabbergasted at the request, I dug her license out to hand it over. (By the way Stella takes a great photo ID.)

He studied it. "What I see here is a cheerful bright person, sparkling blue eyes, with a killer smile. I am going to get you to be like that again. Are you taking any medications?"

I showed him the ER prescribed pain meds list and he looked askance at Stella. "Well, we're going to ditch these. But not all at once, that could make you feel even worse." He asked her to make several movements with her outstretched hands, arms, plus various foot motions the floor, then looked at me. "I will prescribe specific medications, also physical therapy, but I'd like a moment with Stella, if you please."

"Sure." I went into the lobby, bland and beige as most medical suites seem to be, nervously waiting. Frankly, I didn't know what the fuck to think.

Stella came out minutes later, tears in her eyes, clutching a tissue.

"What is it?"

"I've been diagnosed with Parkinson's."

It was a severe gut punch. I felt dizzy and I started to cry, but she stopped me to dab my cheek. "Garrett, only one of us can cry. And I'll be okay."

ONCE WE WERE MAGIC.

ACKNOWLEDGEMENTS

To: **Russell Tumelson** for my first art job when my resume had two entries: Dishwasher and Busboy. **John Saint**, excellent teacher and cupid. **Major General Keith L.Ware** for writing the best Letter of Appreciation I ever got, and will ever get. **Colonel Lloyd S. Sullivan** for trusting a 23-year old behind the wheel of his staff car in DC traffic. **Martin Koble** for bringing that heartwarming electric blanket. **Russ Sacco**, an upstanding roommate and good cook. **Gordon Thomas** who showed me how not to get lost in the Pentagon. **Professors Vic Smith** and **Don Lagerberg**, for seeing me through my BA and MA - particularly **Don** for hiring me the day I graduated. **Steve Johnston**, high school pal, surfing buddy, and 17-year partner at Leysen/Johnston Inc. **Cheryle O'Gara**, terrific ad photographer and email correspondent. **Gene Isaacson** for hiring me at Santa Ana College, and **Estelle Orr** for always assigning the exact classes I wanted to teach. Also at SAC, **Phil Marquez**, Art Chair/Gallery Director, for being a supportive friend, and curating me into exhibitions. Great students (too many to mention), but these spring up - **Joe and Tiffany Perez, Don Simpson, Jennifer Tran, Jason Turnbaugh, Omar Landeros** and **Jay Julos. Sally and Patti** at LACMA ARS Gallery for promoting my work. **Kat Cheema** and **Sharon Berg**, partners at Art Soup LA, for including me on their roster. **Kazumi Inoue**, artist colleague, for volunteering her SUV to drive my larger works. **Ben and Sandy Wright**, congenial, gracious and insouciant hosts of their beachfront Sandy's Sunday Suppers. **Derek** for unbelievable tech-support. And, to bring ONCE WE WERE MAGIC from manuscript to print, many thanks to my editor, **Jeff Edits**. Any mistakes that were due to last minute additions are solely mine, not Jeff's.

ABOUT THE AUTHOR

Artist/author **Mark Leysen** lives with his wife Sherry and son Derek in Irvine, CA. They recently celebrated their 54th anniversary. *Once We Were Magic* is Leysen's fourth novel, and he is currently working on his fifth. Photo of Mark and Sherry taken in 1966.

www.ingramcontent.com/pod-product-compliance
Lightning Source LLC
Chambersburg PA
CBHW020418180626
46812CB00003B/1042